A Second Chance

Chance

SCOTTISH WEREBEARS BOOK 6

LORELEI MOONE

CONTENTS

CHAPTER ONE

This was it, the moment of truth.

James folded his hands and concentrated on keep his breaths even and deep. He was a calm and balanced man normally, but today was different. It was the right thing to do, but he couldn't help worrying about what they would unleash.

Weeks of work would culminate in this one act of rebellion. By the end of tonight, the world would be a different place. They'd be free, or they'd be in more danger than ever before.

He looked around the van where his comrades - his brothers and sisters in revolution - sat. Each of the half dozen of them thoughtful, worried, excited. It was hard to pick just one emotion for tonight. They had worked so hard to make this happen, but there were no guarantees in life. It could all go horribly wrong.

"Five minutes," Henry Weston, their leader remarked, while checking his watch.

Beside him, Gail McPherson - James' former colleague - grabbed Henry's hand, and they shared one of those looks that seemed to speak a thousand words.

Henry cleared his throat, causing everyone else in the back of the van to look up at him.

"You all know this, but I feel it should be said out loud. We've achieved so much in an incredibly short time. Kyle, your internet campaign has made a bigger impact than I ever thought possible," Henry said.

Kyle nodded and looked down at his hands. In the short time James had known him, he'd quickly figured out that Kyle was even more socially awkward than most bears.

"Jamie and Aidan, you've managed to mobilize so many like-minded shifters through the network of contacts you'd built up. Today would not have been possible without your efforts."

The two senior members of the Edinburgh Alliance office exchanged a look and a nod.

James meanwhile rubbed his hands together. So many men and women in such a cramped space meant it was warm, yet his hands had remained cold and clammy.

"James." Henry looked right at him now.

James stopped his fidgeting and looked up again.

"James. The information and support you've provided from inside Adrian Blacke's office has been invaluable. We appreciate the risks you've taken."

James nodded at Henry, who nodded back and checked his watch again.

"The media will have collected outside. We've kept them waiting long enough. It is time."

Henry had barely completed his speech when Heidi, Aidan's mate, turned the handle on the back of the van and gave the door a strong push, causing it to fling open.

Some distance away, lights awaited. These weren't just ordinary streetlights; they were clustered much closer together. TV crews.

"This way," Gail called out.

The group of shifters changed direction and followed her lead, walking at first, then breaking into a sprint. They were going to meet the cameras from a more dramatic angle. As they got closer, the first reporters noticed them and started whispering amongst themselves.

The air was electric. Their campaign had managed to get everyone talking. But nobody knew exactly what was going to happen.

Until it did.

With ten feet to spare, Henry stopped and signaled the rest of the group to do the same.

James stood just towards his left, his breaths short and

quick. He felt his body get ready.

This was something they had never done before. It was forbidden. It was dangerous.

But, it was also necessary.

Henry took one step forward to face the media. "We are the New Alliance."

James closed his eyes as he listened to Henry speak. He thought of his reasons for doing this. Of his sister, Irene, who had first involved him to protect her family.

"You, and the whole world with you, will soon see things you may find hard to comprehend. Understand that we want above all a peaceful coexistence between our species. Do not fear us. Everything will be explained in time." Henry stepped back into line and nodded at Gail, who stood to his right.

The reporters started to whisper among themselves again.

James' skin started to burn and itch. His muscles tensed up. He wasn't just doing this for Irene. He was doing it for himself too. For what he'd given up many years ago.

"Now," Henry spoke in a whisper so low only a shifter could have heard it.

James let his innermost instincts loose. After the first sound of cloth, tearing, the humans that stood in front of them were stunned into silence.

One by one, the shifters transformed. Their group consisted mostly of bears, with a single wolf among them - Heidi.

James took a deep breath, loving the sting of the cold air in his lungs. This was his true nature. It was exhilarating to be able to show it to the world.

They stood proudly in front of the shocked reporters, who seemed frozen in place. Would they run? Would they scream?

Then the first one stirred, touching her earpiece and frowning, while still keeping James and the rest of the group firmly in her sights.

"I understand," the woman whispered. "Yes, it's the same thing here. Yes. I am ready."

She straightened herself and tried to shake off the fear James could smell on her. Then she turned her back on the shifters and faced her cameraman.

"Ladies and gentlemen, as you can see, the spectacle we are faced with here is much the same as on other prominent locations all over the country, as well as the rest of the world. In front of my eyes, these seemingly normal men and women managed to morph into animals. We do not know if they pose a threat, though they announced beforehand that they had no ill will toward us..."

Henry stepped ahead, causing the rest of the confused looking journalists to flinch back a bit.

"We are no threat to you. We simply wish to open a dialogue between your species and ours."

The woman who had been speaking into the camera slowly turned to face Henry. Her eyes were wide with fear.

One of the men behind her started to hyperventilate. "Holy... shit... it can... speak!"

James could hardly contain his concern. This was difficult for any regular human to understand. Would they choose to learn, or would they reject the chance for a peaceful resolution?

"Rachel Kinsey, Sky News," she introduced herself despite the tremble in her voice. "Would you be willing to answer a few questions?"

That was a good start, wasn't it?

"Of course. What would you like to know?" Henry responded.

James tried to listen to the reporter's questions and Henry's answers, but his thoughts were a million miles away. They had actually done it.

After at least a thousand years, the secrecy rules had been broken. They had shown humankind that they weren't the only ones to walk this earth. What happened next was crucial.

James looked around at the other reporters, who were also reluctantly listening in to the interview that was going on just in front of them.

What if the old stories were right? Humans did seem very fearful of what they didn't understand. More so, because they'd ignored an important consideration. One which James had only come to realize now. Even though they spoke of peace and coexistence, they were predators.

A bunch of bears and a wolf.

It was no wonder these people had been scared half to death. Their fear wasn't illogical; it was simply instinct. James' group could tear these humans up in the blink of an eye if they wanted to.

For this reveal, what the New Alliance could have used were some nice cuddly, fluffy animals which humans would feel some sense of endearment towards. But in all their preparations and recruitment up to this point, they had come across only bears, wolves, and the odd fox. James had even heard of a lion and a tiger joining their ranks elsewhere.

Why were there no rabbit shifters?

In the distance, sirens blared. They seemed to be approaching fast. This was their cue.

Henry wrapped up the interview; they gathered up their shredded clothes and scattered as had been agreed in advance. James didn't look back and ran up the hill towards the castle; his agreed escape route.

The fences and barriers were easy for him to climb. Police cars came to a screeching halt further back, presumably where they'd left the reporters. But he wasn't worried. They wouldn't catch him. He ran across the courtyard and climbed the boundary wall. From there he made his way down the hill from the other side, leaving the castle and the cops behind.

Even if they'd just announced their presence to the world, he stuck to his old habits. He chose to stay in the shadows, avoiding any areas where he smelled a human presence. Still, James made good time. He reached his hiding place and quickly pulled out the change of clothes waiting for him. It was much easier to blend into city life if he shifted into his human form again.

So that's what he did. Within minutes, he looked like any other human out for an evening walk. James picked up the messenger bag that had contained his clothes and checked the side pocket. There they were. The keys.

He zipped up his coat and slung the bag around his shoulder. The bunch of keys was now safely in his pocket, though he held on to it tightly just in case.

The wind had picked up, so it took him a while to warm up again in his changed form. The brisk walk helped.

Another five minutes or so and he reached his getaway vehicle. Everything had gone exactly as planned. Still, as he turned the last corner, a strange sensation overwhelmed him. It felt like a presence, like someone had spotted him. But there was nobody around.

He was probably just being paranoid.

James shook off his concerns and pulled out the keys. He'd get in and drive without pause until he reached the New Alliance's hiding place. The city - any city - would be on high alert after the spectacle they had caused. Their faces were out there now. It would only be a matter of time before the authorities would know their identities as well.

Because of this, they had picked a remote location for their hideaway.

The next step was to reconvene; the Edinburgh group would collect in person and communicate with the other factions that had formed all over the country. Together they would decide on their next move.

Tonight had gone reasonably well, but this was only the beginning.

CHAPTER TWO

———◆———

When Charlie reached home, she couldn't wait to get comfortable. She barely even acknowledged her roommate, Ella, as she made a beeline for her bedroom. Finally, after trading her sensible blouse and skirt combo for some warm pajamas and a pair of fluffy socks, she could breathe a sigh of relief.

"Hey you," Ella mumbled when Charlie joined her in the living room again.

"Hey." Charlie frowned as she noticed Ella watching the news. Ella never watched the news. "What's going on?"

Ella briefly glanced at Charlie as she joined her on the couch. "Don't tell me you forgot? It's all over the internet!"

"Well yeah, but don't tell me you believe that crap? *Tonight, your world will change for good.*" Charlie spoke in a dramatic voice. "Nonsense. It'll be a hoax; I'm telling you. They didn't believe it at the Herald either."

Charlie was about to get up again to get something to drink when the newsreader was cut off mid-sentence, and the screen flickered to reveal a red background with the words 'Breaking news' flashing on top.

"We are interrupting your current program with breaking news..."

"See!" Ella exclaimed, and picked up the remote to increase the volume. "No hoax!"

"For the past week, our country, along with the rest of the world, has been in the grips of what some have referred to as the most extensive social media campaign ever. A mysterious organization called the 'New Alliance' has promised us a grand reveal that will change our understanding of the world forever. What exactly this will entail, we do not know. But it better be big, or there is

7 "

likely to be widespread disappointment. Over now to our reporters, who are on the ground in London, Paris, Berlin, even New York on location as communicated to us in advance by this so-called 'New Alliance' ..."

The screen flickered again to reveal a wind-blown man in a suit. "Thank you Shelley, this is Ben Thompson live from London. So far, we have not seen any activity yet."

The view panned to show more of the scenery. Westminster Abbey stood in the background with a busy road in front. Black cabs, as well as the occasional red double decker bus passed by the reporter, but nothing looked out of the ordinary.

"Try another channel," Charlie suggested.

Ella nodded and flipped across a few different channels. On each one of them, a flustered looking reporter stood in a different location around the country, braving the wintry conditions typical for mid-January. They paused on a local channel when they spied a familiar sight, the Royal Mile and a dramatically lit up Edinburgh Castle in the background.

"Wait," Charlie whispered.

She had been skeptical, sure. A healthy amount of suspicion was in her nature. That's what she thought would make her a good reporter one day. How she wished she was there, waiting for the New Alliance to show itself. But clearly, the news channels had taken the announcement seriously enough to disrupt their evening program and dispatch reporters out to various locations all over the world.

Part of her still wondered if it was a prank, even if she secretly hoped that it wasn't. With so many horrible things happening in the world lately; wars, natural disasters, terrible crimes. The prospect of change had seduced many. Even Charlie, with her level head and analytical thought process, hadn't been completely immune.

On the TV, the view changed. No longer was the camera pointed at the Castle, but instead, in the opposite direction. A group of people approached, though they were still too far away to be clearly visible.

Ella picked up a cushion and held it tightly against her chest. Charlie caught herself holding her breath.

Once they were close enough for their faces to be clearly visible, one of the men stepped ahead and started to speak. But Charlie couldn't focus on his words or his features. She was looking at someone just next to him. A familiar face.

Her heart raced, and she broke out into a cold sweat. A face she hadn't seen for years.

All those old memories came flooding back. She was the new girl in school, having only just moved to Stirling that year. The local kids were suspicious of her and kept their distance, at least at first. One made her feel welcome; the boy next door who also happened to be in her school, be it a year above her.

They'd bonded over concerns for the environment and discussions about politics which the other kids were least interested in. He had been an idealist, just like her.

And so they became friends, even if a part of her always knew she wanted to be much more than that. For a year, right up to his graduation, they spent almost every day together.

Suddenly, a certain anxiousness started to grow in her. He was graduating, she wouldn't, not for another year. He would go off to university, and she would be stuck here alone.

He said they'd keep in touch, but she was scared. She couldn't let him leave without following up on those secret desires that had been growing inside of her.

One summer evening, after the graduation ceremony, she mustered the courage. She told him.

He didn't speak, just looked into her eyes.

She stared back.

He closed his eyes. As did she.

They kissed completely on instinct. Thinking back,

Charlie wasn't sure who had made the first move.

It was the best moment of her entire life.

The next day he was gone. He'd left her.

Charlie blinked a few times. Was it really him? He was a few years older now and sported a medium brown neatly kept beard. There was no doubt about it. His eyes were a dead giveaway.

Then, it happened. His features elongated and shifted around. His skin sprouted fur. Within a split second, the boy she'd once known was gone, and in his place stood a great big bear.

"Oh my God!" Ella yelled out next to her and grabbed Charlie's hand. "Are you seeing this? Tell me you're seeing this."

Charlie couldn't speak.

It was him.

James Finch.

She thought she'd never see him again. Wasn't sure if he was alive or dead even, and yet there he was. Despite the otherwise alien form, his eyes were still those same eyes she had known so well. Her best friend. The one who had broken her heart when he left.

The camera panned around and focused only on the slightly bigger bear, who was speaking again.

A talking bear. Charlie shook her head.

It should have shocked her much more, but her mind was still trying to process things. It was as though her chest had been torn open, and her heart ripped out. She ought to have been over the whole thing by now. They were kids back then.

But it hurt like it had happened yesterday.

"What's wrong?" Ella asked.

Charlie didn't respond.

"Why are you crying?" Ella said.

Charlie touched her fingertips against her face, and only now noticed tears had been streaming down her cheeks. She took a deep breath and dabbed at her eyes with her t-shirt.

"Nothing. I'm fine," she mumbled, suddenly angry that this guy could affect her still. He'd left. He hadn't wanted her. End of story.

"Bullshit. That was some freaky stuff we just saw, but that's no reason to cry!" Ella argued.

Charlie shot her a nasty look. "Leave it alone." This was ridiculous. She hadn't cried in years.

"Nuh-uh! You've got to tell me!"

Charlie closed her eyes and shook her head. "Fine. I recognized one of them."

"Oh?" Ella paused. "Oh..."

"Now please leave it." Charlie got up to grab a glass of water from the kitchen.

Ella followed hot on her heels.

"You're kidding. You know one of the New Alliance? That's like... wow. That's so amazing!"

"Yeah. Amazing." Charlie took a sip and brusquely put the glass back down on the counter. Then she just stood there, resting both her hands against the edge of the worktop and stared straight ahead at nothing.

She knew a member of the New Alliance. And he was right here in the city.

Charlie pressed her lips together. She *knew* one of them.

She looked over at Ella, who practically bounced up and down with excitement. "You know what. You're right. It is amazing."

Ella nodded enthusiastically.

"I'm gonna track him down," Charlie said. "I'm going to track him down and get an exclusive interview with him."

Ella clapped her hands and grinned. "Yes!"

"Maybe that'll teach old man Penderton to take me seriously."

"He should!" Ella cheered.

"Maybe then he'll have me work on some *real* stories,

not bullshit cat treat recipes and home remedies for dandruff."

"Good on you!" Ella said. She smiled briefly, then bit her bottom lip. "Say... did you also notice how those guys were all pretty hot?"

Charlie frowned. James had always been a looker, even back in the day when they were awkward teenagers. And whereas the years had made her fill out rather in some unfortunate places, he had piled on muscle from what she could tell. The others, though?

She hadn't even noticed the others. "Mhmm?"

"Well, I was just wondering, if you know... If you track this guy down. And you get to know some of his friends..."

"Yeah?" Charlie asked.

"Well, perhaps you could introduce me. That's all." Ella smiled innocently.

Charlie rolled her eyes. "Whatever. I still have to find him, though."

"Yeah, don't you worry about that. The internet has information about everyone nowadays, and I might know someone who could help." Ella winked at her.

Now, Charlie smiled too. Ella was an avid gamer, and among her rather special group of friends and acquaintances, there was bound to be someone who could help track down James and the rest of the New Alliance. This could work.

Perhaps one day not too far in the future, she would see him again in person. An exciting, though equally scary prospect. How would she face him?

She'd make a list of questions, stuff that people would be desperate to know more about. Just like a good reporter should.

Though she just had one question for him. *Why?*

Why leave like that?

After what she'd seen on TV, it was pretty obvious what his reasons would have been. But she still wanted to hear him say it in his own words. Why couldn't he just tell her then, rather than run?

Ella went back to the sofa and flipped around channels. Each of them, repeated images of different cities, where exactly the same thing had happened as in Edinburgh. Seemingly normal people had approached the waiting journalists and transformed themselves.

Charlie's suspicions had been proved wrong. The 'New Alliance' had done exactly as they'd advertised.

They'd changed the world.

CHAPTER THREE

It was well after midnight by the time James reached the remote farm far north of Edinburgh where they had agreed to gather. All had gone well.

He hadn't been followed; he knew this because the roads were so quiet, there was no way for anyone to do so without drawing attention to themselves.

When he pulled into the long driveway, he saw that there were some vehicles already parked up. Good. So the others had made it as well.

James unlocked the front door and stepped in. Muffled voices greeted him. They were all in the back of the house, no doubt discussing tonight's events.

"Hey," James greeted the first familiar faces. Heidi and Aidan, Henry and Gail; even Kyle was already here.

Jamie, the leader of the Edinburgh branch of the Alliance, was still missing.

"Good show, aye?" Kyle remarked, then focused once again on the TV flickering in the corner. Obviously, they had been watching the coverage.

"That's what I look like?" James mumbled to himself when they showed a still mid-shift. It was unnerving, seeing the transformation captured like this.

Of course, he'd seen other shifters transform, but it was always over so quickly, you couldn't see the process unfold. This right here was the naked truth. And it was quite ungainly.

"Strange, isn't it? We've been working toward this moment, and now it's over," Heidi remarked.

James looked over at her.

"Oh, it's far from over," Henry said. "Now, the real work begins."

James nodded in agreement and sat down on one of

the empty chairs facing the television.

He watched in silence as the news channel showed images from various other locations.

The coverage from Paris took his breath away.

"I've never seen a lion before," Gail gasped, a few seats to his right.

The rest of the group mumbled in agreement.

They had done it. They had changed the world. But was it for the better?

Henry's phone rang; one of the other groups probably. He nodded at Kyle, who got to work immediately. He placed one of those flat conference phones in the center of the group and attached it to a laptop.

James meanwhile continued to watch TV.

"Ready," Kyle said at last.

Henry picked up the remote and dialed down the volume, and he pulled his chair closer to the conference phone.

"Hello? Are you there?"

"Eric from London, here."

"New York. Present."

"Paris."

"Berlin. The Amsterdam group have not yet reached their safe house, but we can speak on their behalf."

"Glasgow."

James' ears perked up hearing his sister's voice. Irene had made it.

"Very good," Henry said. "Let's begin."

Neither James nor the others in his group spoke much throughout the conference call, leaving Henry to do the talking. It was easier that way. They were all on the same page anyway.

They spoke of the human reporters' reactions. Shock, awe, fear. Though apparently in Amsterdam, one of the reporters turned out to be one of their own, who despite not having any previous interactions with the New Alliance had spontaneously decided to join in and shift himself.

They spoke of what to do next. How to demonstrate that they posed no threat to humans. How to educate them.

Kyle, of course, had already prepared the next steps to their internet campaign. An educational website that collected the history as well as important facts about the shifter world. He had even created a mobile game to get the younger generation interested.

All in all, the mood was positive. It seemed that James was the only one with questions. He decided to keep them to himself for now. He didn't want to dampen anyone's spirits.

So as the conference went on, he once again focused on the TV.

The coverage was getting repetitive; the same images kept scrolling past again and again. Until suddenly, the studio came into view.

James wished that the conference was already over, so he could increase the volume to hear what the news anchor was saying. The way she spoke, she was trying to remain professional, but her body language indicated she felt under threat somehow. Then the camera panned do the right and showed the last person in the world James expected to see on TV today.

"Guys. Turn up the TV," James stammered.

Henry shot him a disapproving look. "I'm sorry for my team member here. You were saying, Eric?"

"No, please just trust me on this. See!" James interrupted and pointed at the TV.

Everyone turned their head, and even Henry fell silent for a moment. He grabbed for the remote and increased the volume.

"I'm afraid we'll have to cut this discussion short," Henry said. "Switch on the BBC. You will all want to see this." He pressed the large button on the conference phone and cut off the discussion before anyone else had the chance to react.

"So, Mr. Blacke," the reporter said. "Please state your affiliation to these..."

"Shifters." Adrian Blacke stared into the camera grimly and folded his hands. "I am Adrian Blacke, leader of the shifter world."

"Well, I'll be..." Aidan blurted out.

"What the hell does he think he's doing?" Heidi complained.

"So does this mean you are one of..." The reporter's voice trailed off.

"Yes, I am a shifter. I'll spare you the theatrics. We have seen too much of that tonight already," Blacke responded.

"And you are a part of the New Alliance?"

Henry scoffed at the question.

"No," Blacke almost barked his response. "This so-called *New* Alliance is nothing but a group of troublemakers. I speak for the Alliance. The *real* Alliance. The one that has been around for generations."

"Troublemakers, sir?"

"That's right. They have gone against my orders simply for shock value, they..."

"Shit. This is bad," Gail said.

The group nodded.

"So you were not in favor of tonight's reveal?" The reporter asked, while nervously shuffling around her papers.

"Not at all. Of course, we wish to peacefully coexist with humankind as we have done for many years now. You have nothing to fear. But this was not the way to do it."

"Oh, bullshit!" Aidan growled.

Behind them, the door swung open with a loud creak.

"Late to the party, I see. What did I miss?" Jamie spoke as he marched inside the room.

Nobody said a word, and James just pointed at the TV.

"What the hell is *he* doing on TV?" Jamie wondered aloud, as he pulled up a chair.

"What indeed," Henry said.

"If not like this, how would you have done it?" the reporter asked.

"Well. Firstly, I don't think the timing was right at all. There is enough going on in the world already without adding all this into the mix. There's the conflicts in the Middle East, famines in Africa..."

"What does he know about what's going on in the world? I can bet someone told him to mention these things," James snapped. In all the years he'd worked at Blacke's office, he hadn't known the man to give a hoot about current affairs of the human world. All he cared about was his own position. His power.

The reporter nodded. "But now that everything is out in the open. What if any next steps have you got in mind?"

Adrian Blacke looked up and stared directly into the camera. James felt like he was looking directly at him. "I'll have to manage the hand I have been dealt. Tomorrow I'll travel to Westminster to meet with your government officials. This is a serious matter, and a lot depends on how we manage the transition. In fact, I have already put certain projects in place to help put minds at ease. We are out in the open now. It is in everyone's best interest to ensure that both sides know exactly where they stand."

What projects? He can't possibly be talking about the tracker scheme? James felt his chest tighten with anger. He knew his old boss too well to ignore his words now. If Blacke made a place for himself in London, their efforts in creating the New Alliance and orchestrating tonight's announcement were as good as wasted.

"We can't let this happen." Henry stood up and looked around the room.

James glanced up at him, his expression equally resolute.

"No, we cannot."

"We need to get there before him," Henry said.

"We've been one step ahead of him since we organized ourselves," Gail said. "Let's not start lagging behind now."

"Call Eric. We have much to discuss." Henry gestured at Kyle to get the conference going again.

James got up and went straight for the door. He needed air, more than anything. He needed air, and he needed to think.

Henry would talk to Eric. That was probably wise. Rather than having everyone step into the limelight, it was best if the New Alliance put forth their own leader to take on Blacke in the capital. If those politicians had any sense, they'd see who the better partner would be.

Meanwhile, James had to think about what Blacke was most likely going to do next. He was the one out of the group who knew him the best. He was also probably the one Blacke had felt most betrayed by.

James left the house and broke into a jog. It had started to drizzle while they sat inside. It was pitch black outside. No street lights, no other houses anywhere around. James could see just fine, though. One of the advantages of being a bear.

He made his way into a nearby patch of trees and took a deep breath. He had shifted once tonight already, so he didn't feel much of an urge to do it again. But just the moist, cold air was enough to clear his head.

Blacke only cared about himself. About securing his position and power. So that's what he was likely planning to do in London. He was going to try to make some friends in high places. He now wanted to be known not just as the leader of the Alliance, but the leader of the entire shifter world.

If that meant he had to hand over access to the shifter database he had been trying to build, then so be it.

He would push through his agenda on those infernal tracking devices, as well as the purity nonsense that had sparked the formation of the New Alliance. He would play on people's fears to legitimize his ideas on mixed families.

In the end, Blacke would push for a segregated shifter society, with him at the very top.

With this realization, James took another deep breath and rushed back to the house. If Henry hadn't already figured it out, he had to share his suspicions about what Blacke was planning to do.

CHAPTER FOUR

The morning after the grand reveal, Charlie reached work at eight sharp. The office was already buzzing with activity, and although everyone looked excited, some of her colleagues did seem a bit worse for wear. It was obvious a lot of them had never gone home the previous day.

"I want to know everything, people!" her boss, a rotund grey-haired man named Harry Penderton shouted. "I don't care what you were working on yesterday; today is a brand new day. We need to know where these people came from, how they've been living in hiding for so many years without anyone noticing. We need backgrounds, research, expert commentary. Get to work. There will be no rest for anyone until we have the answers!"

Charlie couldn't suppress a smile as she approached the man. "Sir, I had an idea for a feature,"

"What? Oh, it's you, Charlotte." He adjusted his glasses and looked at her impatiently. "Well, what is it? We haven't got all day."

Just the way he spoke to her had put her off again. Nobody called her Charlotte anymore; not even her folks.

No. She wasn't going to show her hand just yet. "Well. There seems to be some conflict within their ranks. That man, Adrian Blacke said he represented the 'real' Alliance. And that the New Alliance were just troublemakers. It would be interesting to research that angle, don't you think?" Charlie suggested.

Penderton nodded. "Yes. Yes, indeed. Good thinking."

Charlie smiled again. Finally, he liked an idea of hers!

"Goodwin," Penderton called out across the busy office floor. A woman in her mid-thirties looked up from her laptop. "I want to know more about that guy, Adrian Blacke and his Alliance and how the New Alliance fits in."

Charlie's heart sank. He didn't honestly just take her idea and give it to Diane Goodwin?

"But..."

"Yes?" Penderton frowned at her. "We need an experienced journalist on this story. You'll understand."

"So what am I meant to be doing?" Charlie spoke wearily.

"Culture. Human interest. How do they live; what do they eat? You get the drift."

Charlie sighed. Typical. Everyone else was working on the most exciting stories ever, and she would once again be reduced to writing columns about recipes and other inconsequential stuff.

She knew better than to argue, though. Penderton ran a tight ship. He didn't tolerate subordination.

So she would do as she was told, and at the same time go off on her own to get him a story that showed her worth. In this business, you had to show initiative to get ahead.

The only thing she needed was for Ella to call with something tangible...

Charlie looked around the office; her colleagues were scrambling. Those who weren't hunched over their computers researching this brand new phenomena were on the phone, asking anyone and everyone of their usual informants for information about these shape shifters.

They didn't even seem to know where to start.

The moment Ella's contacts would come up with something, Charlie would be miles ahead of the rest of the office. It was hard not to feel a little smug, at least on the inside.

"Boss, I've got a tip," Diane, called out from across the office.

Oh crap, Charlie groaned on the inside. All her optimism had vanished in an instant.

Penderton joined her at her desk immediately. Charlie watched their discussion with bated breath. The story

Diane was now working on had been *her* idea. How in the world had she already found something?

Their hushed voices made it impossible to overhear anything from Charlie's position, so she picked up her mug and approached the coffee maker in an effort to get closer. Of course, this meant she was forced to stand with her back toward them.

"Blacke, yes," Penderton mumbled.

"He will be..." Diane's voice went low again. "Perhaps I can intercept..."

"Good. Go ahead." Penderton said.

Charlie caught herself. She'd been standing here too long with her mug in hand already. Behind her, footsteps dispersed.

She turned and took a sip, before walking back to her desk. Penderton was long gone, while Diane was flitting around her cubicle, packing up her things. Damn. She must have found out something big for Penderton to let her out of the office at a time like this. If only Charlie knew where she was going.

Of course, she couldn't just ask. That would be way too obvious, and she wouldn't get a straight answer anyway.

Charlie sat down behind her desk and started on her own work instead, even if the speculations about Diane's discovery barely allowed her to focus. How did these shifters live? What did they eat? Did they even have their own separate culture, or had they integrated completely into human society?

Where to begin?

Charlie closed her eyes and was greeted with just one image. James.

She had known him so well before he left or so she thought. He seemed like any other teenager at the time. Okay, actually that wasn't quite accurate. But then again, Charlie hadn't been an ordinary teenager either.

Charlie's parents both worked, so they'd mostly hung out together at her place or gone out to the park. But she'd met his parents, briefly, and although they were the sort of people who kept to themselves and didn't socialize much with the rest of the neighborhood, they hadn't seemed too unusual either.

If he was a shape shifter, that meant that his parents were too, right? It *was* hereditary, surely?

Charlie opened her eyes and started to take notes of everything she thought she knew about James and his family. There were precious few facts and a lot of conjecture.

Considering she had had no idea about his true nature until last night, she probably never knew him very well after all.

She sat back in her chair and looked over her list.

Outdoorsy, fit, loner, massive sweet tooth, protective, quiet - except with her...

And it went on. All this was just stuff she remembered about *him*, though. She couldn't simply assume that every one of them shared the same traits, could she?

Charlie flinched when her phone buzzed on top of her desk, the otherwise inconspicuous sound resonating and multiplying against the laminated wood. She checked the display. Ella.

Hell yeah!

She looked around to see if she might be overheard, then answered it as quickly as she could.

"Hey, what have you got?" Charlie said.

"Easy, tiger! How about a 'hello' first?" Ella teased on the other end.

"All right. Hello. Happy now?"

"Ask me how I am."

"Oh come on! You have no concept of the kind of day I've been having so far."

"It's only ten; how bad could it have been?" Ella quipped.

"Get to the point. You wouldn't be calling me unless you've got something, right? And you're making this as painful as possible, so whatever it is, it's good, yes?"

Ella chuckled. Charlie tightened her grip on the phone so much her knuckles turned white.

"Okay, I'll tell you. Remember Todd? Well, he managed to find out that a certain someone you know booked a flight into London early this morning."

Charlie let go of her phone, holding it tightly between her shoulder and side of her head instead and found a fresh page on her notepad. She scribbled down what Ella said as fast as she could. James. London. Early flight.

"Did he travel alone?" Charlie asked.

"Nope. Two others."

"Okay, that all?"

"They rented a car," Ella said. "I'll send you the details."

"Cool. I totally owe you!"

"We'll be even once you introduce me to those guys, yeah?"

"Okay, whatever." Charlie hung up and stared at her phone for a moment. This was it. Soon she'd have her chance to show these people what she was really made of.

"Charlotte," Penderton's voice brought her back to reality. "What's that you've got there?"

Charlie grabbed her notepad and held it up closer to her face; just out of view from where he stood.

"I've been working on what you said, boss. Researching their culture." Charlie looked up at him and forced a smile. The last thing she needed was to be grilled.

"Good. Found anything?"

Charlie remembered the list of supposed shapeshifter qualities she'd noted down based on her interactions with James. "They seem to be a lot like us, sir. Not very exciting."

Penderton nodded and scratched his chin. "Very well. Keep digging."

Charlie felt her grip on the pad tighten. She intended to keep digging, but couldn't do much about it while she sat here at this desk. Meanwhile, Diane was out and about making actual progress.

He was about to turn and walk off again when she spoke up again.

"I may have tracked down someone who knows more about their habits and traditions. Would it be okay for me to go interview them?"

Penderton raised an eyebrow. "You want to go into the field? As a junior reporter? This is highly irregular. If this-"

"Look, I don't know if this person is for real, and I don't want to waste anyone's time. I'm sure everyone else has more important things to work on..." Charlie smiled again, hoping to high hell it looked as innocent as she intended.

"Fine. But you come back with something, you hear?"

Her heart skipped a few beats. He had actually let her follow up on a fictional lead. This was major, and no doubt inspired only by necessity. The others *were* too busy to go on a wild goose chase after what he probably assumed was a nonsense tip anyway. Baby steps.

"Yes, sir. I will."

Charlie packed up her things just like Diane had done earlier. This was her chance to make an impression, and she wasn't going to waste it. If she hurried to the airport, she could catch one of the afternoon flights to London herself. And then...

Crap, would she need a passport? No, she wasn't leaving the country so any form of ID would do...

Her heart was racing now. This was a massive risk. Penderton had allowed her to leave, but that didn't mean she had a travel budget. Any expenses would come out of her own pocket.

Charlie grabbed her bag and took a deep breath before racing out of the office. She could feel her colleague's eyes on her as she left. She was the rookie. Her early departure would spark a lot of speculation and gossip.

Let them talk, Charlie thought when she reached the

elevator. What do they know?

Instead of worrying about her reputation anymore, she checked her wallet. She had a twenty and some change. That was all. In the compartment behind her driving license and unused gym membership card awaited the one thing that would make her crazy plan possible. Charlie retrieved the carefully wrapped up little packet and peeled away the sticky tape that sealed it.

After making the final payment last year, she had promised herself not to use it unless it was absolutely necessary.

The blue and white logo greeted her like an old friend. Charlie checked her watch. There was no other way to get to London on time. She had to hurry. She had to find James.

She had no choice but to use her emergency credit card.

CHAPTER FIVE

James looked out the window as they drove through Central London. Red double decker buses, black cabs, and famous landmarks greeted him.

He had never expected to be invited along on Henry's trip to London to meet with human government officials. In fact, he would have preferred for himself as well as the rest of his group to stay home as planned. They were courting danger; as they'd checked in for their flight, he was certain they'd get caught.

But Blacke was here too, doing the exact same thing, potentially with a head start. And James knew Blacke the best out of everyone in the New Alliance. He was the one most likely to predict his behavior.

So he'd agreed to make the trip. And so far, it seemed that the human authorities hadn't caught on to them yet.

The local New Alliance leader Eric had done his part and set up a meeting with his local Member of Parliament; he was a constituent after all. But that wouldn't be enough. Blacke would be planning to meet with someone much more important, and they had to somehow achieve the same.

As they drove along Whitehall, James just about managed to take a peek into Downing Street, where the Prime Minister's residence and office was. So this was it. The center of the human power structure.

It was a far cry from the comparatively modest and small Alliance HQ in Stirling where James had worked for years. Sure, the Stirling mansion was impressive, but it was just one building. These people had an entire borough dedicated to the government it seemed.

The security around this part of London was equally impressive. Armed police guarded important streets and buildings. Did it always look like this? Or was it due to last night's big reveal that security had been stepped up? Were they perhaps on the lookout for James and the other occupants of this otherwise inconspicuous rental car?

James had never been to London before. Still, his mind refused to stop analyzing what he saw.

No doubt this was exactly the reason Henry had asked him to come along.

James glanced at his fellow passengers. Henry, Gail, and Eric looked determined. They were working towards one firm goal: get some kind of deal with the government in place before Blacke managed to do the same. Or at least minimize any damage Blacke was going to cause.

As they came up to Westminster, their expressions changed, except perhaps Eric's. He looked ahead with the same stoicism he had shown throughout. The others showed awe more than anything. James followed their line of sight.

Ahead stood Westminster Cathedral; a building he'd only seen before on TV. It was beautiful. As were the Houses of Parliament beyond. How many people came here, just like them, hoping to make a difference? How many had succeeded?

He preferred not to dwell on it. Instead, he pulled out some notes he'd made on the flight over. Blacke's likely talking points and strategy. They had to somehow find someone with enough influence to stop any of this from happening.

The last thing any of them wanted was for Blacke to trade his precious tracker program for the promise of power here. All they'd worked so hard to achieve would be wiped out if Blacke was successful. They wouldn't be free but just controlled by another master.

Eric pulled over into a nearby bus stop to let his passengers out.

"Go on inside. I'll join you once I find a place to park," he said.

Henry shook his hand and stepped out onto the pavement, Gail opened her door and followed. James, meanwhile, got out from the roadside and joined his comrades once Eric had pulled away, but not before stealing a glance up in the opposite direction. Big Ben towered over them from the other side of the road. This was a very strange place. Very humbling.

The three of them didn't waste any more time. They had an appointment with a Conservative Member of Parliament. And hopefully that would be just the first step.

———— ♦ ————

The meeting with the MP had gone well. While Henry had done most of the talking at first, but when the time came to explain Blacke's background, James had taken over.

And the man himself, Oliver Teese, who had started off visibly reluctant to hear them out, had been won over. He was going to help them and take this up the chain. Not out of the goodness of his heart of course; James was certain he was just trying to gain points with more senior members of his party.

Clearly, Politics worked much in the same way everywhere, whether inside the Alliance or out of it.

Either way, the short meeting they'd had had paved the way for bigger, better things. But it wouldn't be until the next day before they had their meeting with the Home Secretary's aides, and then perhaps the woman herself.

"Good job," Henry said as they made their way towards the Central Lobby of the House of Commons. "We've made some real progress today."

James nodded. He still could hardly believe that the three of them had just been allowed inside to meet with someone, without much security at all. Sure, they had been searched, and passed through a metal detector on the way in. But considering their special abilities, that was hardly enough. A shifter even without weaponry posed much more of a risk than these humans seemed to realize.

All it took was one bad apple to ruin it for all of their kind. Surely that wasn't was Blacke was planning; he'd be way too keen to come to a diplomatic arrangement of some sort. But if it didn't work out... Was Blacke crazy enough to initiate an attack if things didn't go his way?

James wasn't sure.

And so he remained thoughtful and quiet, keeping his eyes on the floor, while Henry and Eric discussed the meeting in more detail beside him.

"Something wrong?" Gail, who had been similarly quiet, finally asked him.

James looked up at her. "Nothing. It's a lot to take in." He did have a nagging feeling that something significant was about to happen though. But it wasn't tangible enough to mention it to anyone, not even Gail - his former colleague from the Alliance HQ.

She nodded. "If all goes well tomorrow, we'll be well placed against Blacke."

He had to agree.

They walked on towards the exit when a figure caught his attention from the corner of his eye.

"James," a female voice called out to him. "James Finch."

He instantly froze. He knew this voice from a long time ago.

James turned around. There she was; a ghost from his past.

Charlotte McAllister blinked a few times, but maintained eye contact from the moment he'd noticed her. Those bright, intelligent eyes seemed to bore right into him, uncovering his deepest, most secret desires.

"Yes," he responded, more out of reflex than anything else.

It was unmistakably her, though there was something different that didn't match up with his old memories. Something in the way she looked at him had changed. Her eyes were colder, more guarded now than they used to be.

Of course, you idiot. You shared a kiss and abandoned her. Of course she's going to be different now, so many years later.

"Your presence here has been leaked to the media. They're all waiting outside," Charlotte nodded towards the main entrance halfway across the hall they currently found themselves in.

Henry cleared his throat and shot James a concerned look. "Friend of yours?"

He turned to face Charlotte and continued. "Anyway, we're not opposed to speaking with the media, but we prefer to do it on our terms. Now is not the time."

"Well, I can show you another way out, then you can avoid them." Charlotte smiled at Henry briefly, then continued to stare at James.

It had occurred to James that going public himself could have unforeseen consequences. But he'd had no way to predict a reunion with the one person from his past who could have changed his entire life. At the time, it seemed like the right thing to do. But as soon as he found out that his own sister had taken a human mate... He'd often worried that he'd made a huge mistake.

"Fancy seeing you here," James mumbled.

Charlotte frowned, then turned on her heel and started walking. "This way if you want to avoid the craziness outside."

Henry, Gail and Eric didn't waste time and left James behind scratching the back of his head. Was this a coincidence? He wasn't sure he believed in coincidences when it came to relationships.

He forced himself into motion and caught up with the rest of his group just as they entered a small corridor that veered left from the main hall. There they passed by the cloakroom and bathroom facilities, before ending up at a doorway to the outside world flanked by two guards who barely took notice of their departure.

Outside, the wind had picked up, but there was no sign

of much activity - press or otherwise.

"Which way to the car?" Gail asked.

Eric took a moment to look around, before seemingly finding his bearings.

"Thank you very much, miss ..." Henry offered Charlotte his hand, who shook it without hesitation or fear.

"McAllister. Charlie McAllister," Charlotte said.

Clearly she knew who they were. But if the events of last night had made any sort of impression on her, she wasn't showing it.

"Yes, thanks," Gail said with a smile.

Eric had already wandered off to find the car, leaving just James to say goodbye to her.

Only... he didn't really want to.

He never expected to see her again, not after what had happened between them when they were only teenagers. Back then he had felt forced to leave her behind, but for what? Those uncertainties and concerns were the exact thing the New Alliance aimed to destroy.

Now, as he found himself once again looking into those endless blue eyes of hers, he wondered how things might have turned out, had he made a different choice back then.

"How about you guys go ahead," James mumbled.

Gail cocked her head to the side as she looked at him.

Henry frowned. "Are you sure?"

"I'll catch up with you at the house later," James added.

Henry opened his mouth to say something else, but didn't. Instead he exchanged a look with Gail and his expression softened.

The New Alliance counted a number of mated couples among its ranks, still the whole non-verbal communication trick they all seemed to know never ceased to amaze James.

"Very well. I'll hear from you. We have a lot to prepare for." Henry nodded at James and offered Gail his arm.

They didn't look back as they walked off in the same direction as Eric, who had long since turned a corner and passed out of view.

"You don't want to go with your friends?" Charlotte asked.

Her tone was matter-of-fact, business-like, though he thought he could catch a hint of the dry humor he'd loved about her in the past.

"They'll be fine. We have a lot to talk about, you and I," he responded.

They were alone. He'd often wondered about what he might say if he ever met her again. Though right now, he couldn't remember any of the words he'd chosen for just this occasion.

"Do we?" Charlotte raised an eyebrow.

"How about we find somewhere quiet? Have lunch?" he suggested.

She looked back at the figures of Henry and Gail who had become smaller and smaller. "Why not? I have to admit I'm curious."

CHAPTER SIX

Charlie had taken the first available flight to London City. It was a risk, especially if it didn't work out. Penderton would be furious if she stayed away too long without anything to show for it, and worse, she'd have that credit card bill to worry about come next month.

But Charlie was confident about Ella's tip. It all made perfect sense. Assuming James and his people had no idea about Adrian Blacke's plan to talk to someone in government until his TV appearance, they would be scrambling to do the same thing. And that's exactly where Charlie would go to try to intercept them; Westminster. Luckily, she knew her way around the place a bit from previous visits.

Can't become a serious journalist without ever having visited the seat of government, as her Dad had said when they'd made the trip together a few years ago.

When she reached the public entrance to the House of Commons, she'd spotted her rival, Diane, waiting outside already. That's when her competitive juices had started to flow.

She wasn't about to watch her one chance at a big story fall to pieces because Diane-bloody-Goodwin got to these bear people first.

So she found another way inside the building and waited. It wasn't long before they appeared. A perfect coincidence? She could have so easily missed them, had she reached it only a few minutes later.

When she saw James enter the large hall with three others, her feet barely wanted to move. How would she face him? Then again, all that was in the past. They were kids back then. Surely she was over it?

So she forced herself into action and stopped them.

And from the second she did, she couldn't take her eyes off James. The grainy images on TV hadn't done him justice. What she saw was far removed from the boy she'd known years ago; he had grown into so much more than that. And he kept looking at her too.

No matter how hard she tried to remain professional, her impulses were hellbent on trying to betray her.

When he sent the others away and asked to have lunch with her, she knew she shouldn't say yes. She'd lose herself if she spent too much time with him alone. But saying no wasn't an option either. Her heart hadn't permitted it.

And so she found herself sitting opposite him in a quaint little bistro, pretending to study the menu, without being able to focus on any of it.

She had to get herself under control somehow. This wasn't how a serious journalist was meant to behave!

"Are you ready to order?" The waitress looked disinterested, tapping her foot impatiently while making a show of holding up her notepad and pen in front of her.

"Roast beef on whole wheat and a latte," James said.

"All right. And for you?" the girl asked.

Charlie's mind was completely blank. She wasn't even hungry. "Uhh... Same thing please."

The waitress vanished immediately, leaving Charlie alone with James.

"Having second thoughts?" he asked. His voice sounded like he was grinning.

Yes, definitely, Charlie thought. Then she realized she was still staring at the menu and forced herself to put it down. She took a deep breath, but her heart refused to calm itself.

"I imagine you have questions," James remarked.

She stared at him again. Those brown eyes. She had missed them. She had missed him.

"You hurt me," Charlie blurted out, then immediately covered her mouth with her hand.

James averted his gaze. His expression had gone from

cheerful to dead serious in an instant.

"I'm sorry, Charlotte."

The hairs on her arm stood up when he said her name.

"It's Charlie."

He looked up again. She knew it would be difficult to see him again, but this was excruciating.

She wanted to be angry with him, blame him for breaking her heart at the tender age of sixteen. But the moment he made eye contact with her, she just couldn't muster any anger.

"Charlie... I really am sorry. At the time I felt that I didn't have a choice," James whispered.

"Because of... the bear thing," Charlie said.

He nodded. "We have rules - *had* rules. Our kind has been keeping our existence a secret for centuries, perhaps even millennia."

"Until yesterday."

"That's right."

This was it. These were the sort of insights Penderton would salivate over. This conversation could put her name on the front page.

Charlie pressed her lips together. No matter what had happened between them, could she live with herself if she wrote all this up behind his back?

"Things have been difficult lately. There's this guy, who thinks of himself as the leader of our kind-"

"Adrian Blacke," Charlie said. This was wrong. She shouldn't push him for information without disclosing who she was first.

James sat back in his chair. "That's right. He's power hungry and dangerous. A lot of lives hung in the balance, and coming out publicly was the only way we saw to keep people safe."

This was major. If this Blacke fellow was as dangerous as James said he was, the world had a right to know. Especially if he was trying to make some kind of deal with the government! People needed to know who they were dealing with.

"Frankly, I never thought I'd see you again," James said.

Charlie felt the sting of tears in her eyes.

"But I'm glad that I have." He reached across the table for her hand.

When his index finger touched hers, it was like an electric current passed through the two of them. It took her breath away, and she flinched, pulling away her hand immediately.

This was too much. How was it even possible that after all these years he still had such a profound effect on her? How could she be so stupid, so juvenile Perhaps Penderton was right not to let her work on anything serious yet. She clearly wasn't professional enough.

"Charlie," James said.

His low voice sent shivers from the nape of her neck all the way down her spine. "Yes?"

"Have you ever wondered *what if*?"

That question, perhaps innocently posed, finally set off her anger. "Are you kidding me? The day after we kissed, I went looking for you. You were gone; your whole family was gone, leaving behind an empty house! I was sick over it. Don't even know how I managed to survive the next year on my own and graduate. I thought of nothing *but* what-ifs. If only I'd kept my feelings to myself. Perhaps we still would have been friends. I wouldn't have lost the one person in my life who meant the most to me!"

Charlie's eyes were filled with tears now. Tears of anger.

"I had no other choice. The moment I figured out you felt the same, I knew I wouldn't be able to stop myself if I stayed in touch. It would have put both of us, and my family, in an impossible situation."

Charlie shook her head.

Meanwhile, the waitress arrived with their order, causing a painful silence between them. Charlie turned away to disguise the fact that she was crying. She definitely wasn't hungry now. And the thought of coffee turned her stomach.

"Tell me, if you'd seen back then what you saw on TV last night, how would you have taken it?" James asked. His tone was flat, like he wasn't arguing, but had already admitted defeat.

Charlie picked up a stray piece of rucola off her plate and put it in her mouth. Its sharp, peppery taste seemed to ground her a little.

Wait, what was his question?

She stared at him again even though her vision had become blurry.

"I don't know. I don't even know what to think now." She really didn't. Seeing James again had shocked her to her core, so much so that the whole bear situation seemed comically surreal and far-fetched.

James nodded and looked down at his own sandwich.

"It's a lot to process. I thought leaving was my only option at the time. Now I'm not so sure." He pushed his plate away and rested his elbows on the table.

Charlie tried to process everything he'd said. If only she'd had the presence of mind to record it, like a real reporter. In all her confusion, she must have missed most of his words. *Dammit*, she'd forgotten all about that list of questions she'd carefully prepared in the plane earlier today as well!

"Charlie," he said, but she didn't react. "Charlie," he spoke louder this time, causing her to flinch and focus on his eyes again. The tenderness and emotion she saw in them almost made her cry again.

"What if this is fate? What if we were meant to meet again after all this?"

Charlie frowned. She had never known him to be the sort of guy to believe in *fate*. And she wasn't sure she did either.

"What are you trying to say?" she asked.

"This is my chance to make it up to you. And then, who knows? Perhaps we could try again?" he asked. His eyes had widened now; he had gone from remorseful to excited and full of hope.

Charlie couldn't believe her ears, neither could she keep up with his strange, mixed signals. The wounds he'd left were still too fresh, despite the years that had passed in between. And when she'd decided to track him down, getting a second shot at a relationship with him had been the last thing on her mind. No, she was here to get a story. Perhaps some closure as well.

An apology and short explanation about how they were supposed to live in secret wouldn't do. It wasn't enough to rebuild what they'd lost.

James had been the only guy she'd ever allowed close to her, and it had backfired spectacularly. His disappearance had made her swear off love and go down a different path for herself. He was the reason she'd gone out on her own and made a career for herself.

Charlie shook her head. This wasn't how today was supposed to go.

"Think it over," James said, with a twinkle in his eye.

He pulled his plate closer again and picked up the sandwich.

No way. She didn't know quite how to respond.

And anyway, he wouldn't have said that if he knew why she was actually here. This time, he wasn't the one with the secret, she was.

"You've got some guts," Charlie mumbled, as she watched him take a big bite of his lunch.

"You have no idea," he responded.

Behind them, some of the other customers started speaking up.

"Hey, someone, can you turn that up?" someone said.

"Yes, turn it up!" Another customer chimed in.

Charlie turned around to find a group of city people in suits, crowding around the counter to watch the TV on the wall.

The bored looking waitress picked up the remote and increased the volume enough so Charlie could hear.

"The latest development in the New Alliance reveal... Our reporter, Rachel Kinsey is in the field."

"Oh bloody hell," James mumbled. "It was only a matter of time before those people got involved."

Charlie turned to find him staring in the direction of the TV with a horrified expression on his face.

CHAPTER SEVEN

Things had been going so well between the two of them, James thought. And then, just like last night, a single TV appearance changed everything.

As James watched the coverage of one reporter's visit to an anti-shifter protest in Glasgow, a sort of catharsis washed over him. This completed the list of players.

The New Alliance, as well as Adrian Blacke and his people, had always shared an enemy. The Sons of Domnall were getting in on the action.

The camera panned across hundreds of people who had gathered in Glasgow's city center. Some were carrying placards with slogans; others held up pictures of what James presumed were loved ones who had been captured or eliminated by the Alliance over the years. It was a scarily one-sided picture, which would no doubt sway public opinion against the New Alliance and the shifter world.

A middle-aged man with salt and pepper hair stepped up onto a makeshift podium and started addressing the crowd, as well as the camera. Underneath him on the screen appeared a white banner with a name that made James do a double-take. Victor Domnall, leader of the Sons of Domnall. In all the years the Alliance had fought against the Sons of Domnall, they had never seen or heard of an official leader. It seemed that the reveal had inspired everyone else to embrace transparency too.

"For too many years, we've struggled against these monsters in the shadows. For too many years, we have sacrificed our sons and daughters for the safety of the human race. It is time for our fight to enter the limelight. These *shifters-*" he spat out the word and made the quotation mark gesture with his fingers, "They talk of peace and harmony, but you've seen their claws. Their sharp teeth. They are not our friends. There is a reason ancient man hunted the predators of the animal kingdom to extinction in these parts. To keep our families safe. Just because these mutants have evolved some form of higher intelligence and the ability to disguise themselves as humans, does not change their true nature. In fact, it makes them all the more dangerous. They are beasts, meant to be conquered and tamed. We are The Sons, and our resistance serves you all."

James glanced at Charlie who sat across from him. She was intently watching the screen and didn't take notice of him. The rest of the customers in the cafe did the same. This man was bloody convincing; a brilliant orator. Just with those relatively few words, he might have swayed some of these people into supporting his cause.

The Sons of Domnall had always operated in secret, simply because most people probably wouldn't have believed in shifters unless they had seen one themselves. Now, this was no longer necessary. Except for those inevitable few who thought the reveal had been some kind of hoax or conspiracy, most people believed.

It wouldn't be difficult for the Sons to start recruiting new members. Not just those fringe elements of society who were suspicious of outsiders by nature, but regular, sensible people, who couldn't see past the predator exterior of the shifters.

The New Alliance had to step up their efforts to appeal to common people, or they would lose this battle before it had even begun.

This wasn't a holiday. He had accompanied Henry and Gail to London for serious work, not fun and games. Now, it was time to get back to it.

"I have to go," James said, while he fumbled with his wallet, leaving a few notes on the table to cover their lunch.

"What?" Charlie turned around.

"I have to get back to my people."

She looked at him in silence. Those bright blue eyes of hers could capture him just as they had done so many years ago. She finally nodded.

"Can I have your number?" she asked.

James smiled. "Only if I can have yours."

His heart meanwhile hammered away in his chest; as hard as he tried to cover it up, he couldn't ignore the danger they faced. The speech they'd just watched was a ticking time bomb. They couldn't afford for the Sons to gain momentum now while they were most vulnerable.

She scribbled her digits on a piece of paper. Meanwhile, he did the same.

"You'll get back okay?" James asked.

She hesitated for a moment and smiled awkwardly. "Yeah, no problem."

Her response gave him pause. "That didn't sound convincing."

"Yeah, no, it'll be fine." Charlie put the note with his phone number into her wallet, which she stuffed into the shoulder bag she'd been carrying.

"You don't live here in the city, do you?" James sat back and observed her.

She slowly shook her head.

"Do you have anywhere to stay?" he followed up his question.

She kept her gaze locked on the leftover sandwiches on the table between them and shook her head again.

James' protective instincts kicked in. He couldn't very well invite her along to Eric's place, but he could make sure that she was safe and comfortable.

He pulled out his wallet again and took out a few notes.

"Whoa, I don't want your money!" Charlie protested.

"Just find yourself a decent hotel somewhere at least!" James insisted.

She looked at the money and up into his eyes again. "I'll pay you back."

James smiled. "Sure. If that's what you want."

"Yes, that's what I want," Charlie spoke resolutely.

She finally accepted the money, her fingers brushing past his in the process. The first time they'd touched, the sensation had been intense. This time, it was even stronger.

James looked into her eyes and knew she felt it too.

Everything seemed to be falling apart around them, and yet his instincts told him to make her his. Of course, she hadn't forgiven him for what he'd done; for leaving her. He hadn't forgiven himself either.

James couldn't stop his mind from racing as they said their goodbyes. He wasn't sure how they'd ended up running into one another today, in what seemed to be a strange city for both of them. It had to be fate, as silly as that sounded.

She represented his one regret in life. He'd never even looked at another woman the way he was looking at her now.

They nodded at each other awkwardly and mumbled their goodbyes. Just as well they hadn't shaken hands or hugged; he wouldn't have been able to let her go.

This wasn't goodbye. He was certain he'd see Charlie again, and he wouldn't have to wait for ten years this time.

———•◆•———

"Henry," James greeted his leader as the latter opened the door to Eric's flat.

"James. We have a lot of work to do."

James nodded and stepped inside.

"You've seen the Sons protest?" James asked. The flickering TV in the corner of the living room suggested his question was superfluous.

"He was good, wasn't he?" Gail, who sat on one of the sofas, asked. "I still can't believe we'd never heard of this guy..."

"Yes, he was. Their rhetoric has always been seductive.

A certain proportion of the populace will identify with it." James took off his coat and pulled up a chair.

"You know what they say," Henry said. "Know your enemy."

Except for Henry, Gail, and Eric, there were a few new faces in their midst. Members of the London crew.

"So what's our next step?" Eric asked, looking at Henry expectantly.

"Our plan has been to educate from the start. We'll have to step it up if we want to avoid pushing people towards the Sons."

"They had names, pictures. Do we have a list of our own?" James asked. "I know we had some files over at Blacke's office of deaths and abductions which potentially linked back to the Sons, but they were far from complete."

Henry leaned forward and rested his chin on his hands. "The Glasgow office certainly did when I was in charge. I'm pretty sure the Edinburgh office had quite a collection too. I'll check in with Jamie." He sat up straight again and looked in Eric's direction.

"Can you reach out to anyone you might know in the London Alliance for this information? Perhaps someone who might be on the fence about whether to continue following Blacke? If the Sons ramp up their activities, it'll be bad for all of us anyway."

Eric nodded and got up to make the call.

James, meanwhile, pulled out his notes on Blacke and started to strategize. Education was definitely the only way forward. "How's our web campaign doing?" he asked.

"I'll get Kyle's report within the hour," Henry responded.

"And we might as well bring all this up tomorrow," James suggested. Whatever happened, they still *did* have a meeting with the Home Secretary's people in the morning.

"Actually, what we need the most," James thought aloud, "is a face. Someone with real skin in the game. Someone who has lost someone perhaps... Someone sympathetic."

James looked up at Henry, who returned his gaze. "Alison," both spoke together.

"Do you think she'll be up for it? She'd have to go public about her involvement with Jamie," James said.

Henry shrugged. "Only one way to find out."

"Why just her? How about the whole family? Jamie and especially his brother Matthew have quite a story to tell." Gail suggested from across the room.

James didn't know them too well, so he had no way of predicting if they'd be up for this. But the Brown child abduction case was well known in their circles. If they could somehow get Alison on record to speak about why she switched sides, and Matthew to share his experiences being kidnapped as a child and growing up in a strange environment without his brother and his parents... Perhaps they could even involve the parents as well!

That would make for an amazing story; one few people could simply brush away.

The truth was, there was heartache and loss on both sides, but the Sons had forced the shifter world to protect themselves by any means necessary. This was another reason why coming out into the open had been the only way forward. They had to stop the endless cycle of violence and hate somehow.

"That could work," James finally said. "We do need a way to legitimize our story, though. If we simply post it on our website, the Sons will brush it away as propaganda and lies."

"We need to do it through the mainstream media," Henry agreed.

"Meanwhile, what do we do about Blacke?" James asked, remembering the original problem that had brought them to London in the first place.

What followed were many more hours of intense discussion and brainstorming which left James exhausted. He - like most bears - wasn't used to this much talk.

They'd made progress, though. By the end of it, they had a list of talking points for the morning as well as a plan for making shifters seem more sympathetic. If it came down to it, they could even blame all the violence on Blacke. The conflict between the Sons and the Alliance had escalated under his watch after all.

It was one in the morning when James finally retired to the cramped room he shared with one of the London guys. Although exhausted, sleep didn't find him yet. Instead, he got out his phone and the piece of paper Charlie had given him. Her phone number.

He wanted to call her, or at least send her a message. It was too late, though. He'd only disturb her.

So instead he just stared at her handwriting. It had hardly changed in all those years.

When he closed her eyes, he could still catch her scent.

The man in the bed across the room started to snore, but James was still up. He had meant what he said to her. If she gave him the chance, he would do anything to fix things between them.

His whole reason for leaving her no longer existed. The secret was out.

Their chance meeting had been a sign. He was sure of it.

CHAPTER EIGHT

Ever since checking into her hotel, Charlie had felt restless. She had settled down on the bed and switched on the TV but couldn't focus on any of it.

What was she doing here?

Sure, she'd found James and spoken with him. She'd even managed to glean some insights into the current events and the reasons behind the New Alliance reveal. Perhaps that would be enough to pacify Penderton and guarantee she kept her job once she got back to the office. He'd let her out of the office to follow a lead, but she'd been gone an entire day already. By now, he'd be furious.

But she couldn't in good conscience report back on it behind James' back, could she?

Why not, actually? Why did she still have this sense of loyalty towards him when he had simply abandoned her a decade ago?

Just thinking about it made her sick. No matter how stupid and weak it made her feel, she couldn't betray him. The next time she saw him, she had to come clean.

Finally, after staring at the ceiling for an hour or so, her lids became heavy. She drifted off into a restless slumber. And even now, the memories of her lunch with James didn't leave her alone. She kept seeing him in her mind's eye. The way he looked at her. The way he spoke of second chances.

And finally, the way he'd left in a hurry after that weird man had appeared on TV.

"We'll meet again," she heard him say. "I'll find you. You're mine."

Those last words filled her with an overwhelming warmth. Yes. She wanted to be his. She wanted to kiss him again and so much more.

It had felt so good; that one kiss they shared ten years ago. If there was ever a moment in her life when everything was perfect, that had been it. She wanted to feel that way again. Excitement to the point of giddiness. Butterflies filling her stomach. And hope. Above all, she wanted to feel hopeful for the future again. That she wasn't meant to stumble through life alone, but that she'd have someone to share everything with.

When she awoke, all was dark around her. The alarm clock on the bedside table read 1:05.

What a dream.

Charlie stretched and turned onto her side. She picked up the phone that lay beside her pillow and stared at it for a moment. She wanted to call him so badly.

Earlier in the day, she'd been conflicted. His presence had reminded her of all those old feelings that still brewed in her. But she'd had trouble ignoring all the pain his disappearance had caused.

Now, after that dream... She just wanted him back.

Should she tell him she'd had a change of heart?

It was late, though. And perhaps this was just a moment of weakness, nothing more.

Charlie sighed deeply and pushed the phone under her pillow. This wasn't the time.

Still, she was awake already. There was no way she could fall asleep again.

So she switched on the light and grabbed her notepad and a pen. Work always provided a good distraction.

Rather than obsess about her feelings, she wrote down everything she'd learned about shifters. They had a dangerous enemy it seemed. The Sons of Domnall. The speech they'd seen at the cafe reminded Charlie of the kind of rhetoric you usually heard from nationalists. It was always *us vs. them*. The familiar vs. the *other*.

There was no doubt that it would appeal to people. She was biased, of course, because she knew James. Other people didn't have that luxury. They'd see teeth and fur and claws and let their most basic instincts take over.

If they wanted to prevent these people from gathering support, they had to show the world another side to the shifters. That there was more to them than their dangerous exterior. That they were human at heart.

Charlie noted down everything in a frenzy. This was exactly the kind of thing she normally did at the Herald. She was used to writing feel-good fluff. No matter how much she'd cursed her assignments in the past, they had taught her how to appeal to people's hearts.

If she had to come clean about her job, and why she'd come to London in the first place, she might as well offer her help. That way, she didn't have to keep secrets from James, and Penderton would be happy too. It was a win-win.

———•◆•———

When Charlie awoke again, it was already morning. Light streamed in through the open curtains, bathing the whole room in a golden glow.

Beside her, pages upon pages of scribbled notes awaited. All this would help her talk to James about her work. She wasn't sure of his schedule today. With a bit of luck, they could have lunch again. Then she'd come clean and explain her plan to help their cause. Once that was done, perhaps she could get on an afternoon flight home so perhaps she could catch Penderton before he went home for the day and grovel her way back into work.

Charlie got up and immediately went in for a shower. Then she tossed her stuff into her messenger bag and made sure none of her belongings were left around the room. If he wanted to meet soon, she was ready to check out already.

Once everything was done, she sat down on the bed and took a deep breath before dialing his number. She let it ring, but there was no answer. The voice mail picked up after a while.

Fine. Perhaps he was busy. She hung up without leaving a message and tapped out a text instead.

Call me when you see this - Charlie

And then she waited.

Nothing. Was something wrong?

She tried calling again, but the same thing happened.

A growing sense of unease descended over her, which she tried to brush away as paranoia. Finally, she switched on the TV to provide some distraction.

The news coverage was mostly the same; repeats of the New Alliance reveal, the hate speech, Adrian Blacke's appearance. The only new thing Charlie saw was an appearance by some university professor who spoke about anthropological evidence of shifters in other cultures. He seemed flustered, as though he didn't want to be on TV at all.

An hour or so later, Charlie couldn't stand waiting around the room anymore. The endless repeats of the same news over and over grated at her. Plus, she'd missed the breakfast buffet and had started to get hungry.

So she picked up her things and made her way towards a quaint little cafe near the hotel. Despite being in a much larger city than what she was used to, this cafe didn't feel strange at all. She watched the world go by from her window seat.

People in suits, rushing to get to work while balancing takeaway cups of coffee and pastries or sandwiches in their hands. There was a bus stop outside, so it was only when one of those red double-decker buses arrived that Charlie could even tell she was in London and not Edinburgh.

A large latte, a danish pastry and a whole lot of people watching later, her phone rang, nearly causing her to jump out of her seat.

It wasn't James, though.

"Hello, Ella," Charlie answered.

"You sound disappointed! Were you expecting

someone else to call?" Ella teased.

"Nevermind. I've not had much sleep," Charlie lied.

There was a pause.

"Anyway, I just wanted to check in to see how things were going..."

Charlie took a deep breath. It would be so much safer to keep everything locked up inside and not tell her anything. But somehow, that same paranoia, or whatever it was, had come back. She needed a release.

"I found him, yesterday," Charlie began.

"Oh! That's awesome! What did he say? Don't tell me that's why you haven't slept much?" Ella's voice had become shrill with excitement.

"We had lunch. That's all. But..." Charlie took a deep breath.

"But?"

"He said he wants to try again," Charlie said. It sounded surreal, hearing those words aloud again.

"Wow! Just like that?"

"Yeah... I don't know what to think. How can I trust him after what happened, you know?"

"Hmm, that's a tough one. I guess you gotta follow your heart on this," Ella said.

"And now today he's not picking up or returning my messages..." Charlie closed her eyes and rested her face in her hands. "I can't shake the feeling that something's wrong."

"I see. Well, perhaps he's just busy," Ella said; her uncertain tone didn't convince Charlie.

"And on top of that, he kept saying about how it was a sign that we bumped into each other..."

"That's... that's rather sweet, actually."

"Right. But it wasn't a coincidence at all, was it? I had tracked him down with your help." Charlie sighed and looked out the window again.

"True..."

"I still need to tell him what I do for a living."

"Oh, shit, Charlie! You had lunch with the guy and kept your job a secret? Don't tell me you wrote about him already!" Ella demanded.

"No, no, of course not! I would never-" Charlie didn't finish that sentence. She had planned to do exactly that; go in, talk to James - ideally record the conversation as evidence - and write an article that Penderton would *have* to put on the front page. Why hadn't she done it? Not out of the goodness of her heart, no. Simply because she wasn't over James, which was worse.

"So... are you going to tell him?" Ella asked finally.

Charlie nodded, though of course, Ella couldn't see it. "Yeah, that's what today was all about. I wanted to meet with him in person and come clean. But now I'm just scared that something has happened."

"Okay."

"What if I don't get that chance, Ella? What if-" Charlie's mind raced with paranoid scenarios that might have prevented James from taking her calls. "He could have been arrested. Or - did you see that strange protest on the news yesterday? What if some of those anti-shifter guys hurt him?"

"Charlie... Charlie!" Ella's tone was firm.

"Yes?"

"You've got to calm down. I'll ask my friend to look into it again. Perhaps we can figure out together what's going on. But give it a day, okay? Don't drive yourself crazy now. Perhaps he was just busy, and all of this will seem silly when he calls back later today."

"Yeah..." Charlie sighed again. She had lost it. Her mind as well as her composure. This was totally unlike her.

"Promise me you'll relax," Ella said.

"Okay. You're right."

"Now... Did you meet any of his friends? Were they hot?" Ella's eagerness made Charlie chuckle despite herself.

"You're impossible!"

"What? I haven't forgotten about our deal. I hope you haven't either, because I'll hold you to it." Ella laughed.

Charlie shook her head and smiled. "Fine! I'll tell you everything..."

55

CHAPTER NINE

The following morning, everyone was up early. James, Henry, and Gail had their appointment at the Home Secretary's office at nine. Meanwhile, Eric was going to meet with someone from the London branch of Adrian Blacke's Alliance. If they wanted to effectively counter the Sons, and get the public on their side, they had to work together.

James couldn't help feeling distracted, though. He hadn't heard from Charlie, and he couldn't wait to call her and perhaps agree to meet again later in the day. In the back of Eric's car, he kept peeking at his phone every so often. It was perhaps still a bit early; maybe she wasn't up yet. He should contact her later, after the meeting.

When he put his phone back in his pocket for the fourth time, he noticed Gail observing him.

Henry, who sat in the passenger seat, immediately turned and looked at him too.

"James, I didn't want to bring this up before the meeting, but perhaps it's best to get this over with."

James frowned. What was he talking about?

Henry and Gail exchanged a look.

"Your friend, Charlotte McAllister..." Gail spoke softly.

"What about her?" James asked.

"It was strange, how she just happened to be there yesterday to tip us off about the media waiting by the main entrance." Henry cleared his throat.

"A lucky coincidence," James said.

"Right. Well, I had Kyle do a bit of digging..." Henry said.

James felt his muscles tense up. Henry checked up on his woman? How dare he! He took a deep breath and remained silent, waiting for what more Henry would say. If he apologized, James still wouldn't be happy, but he'd keep quiet about it. Henry was the boss, after all.

"She's a reporter, James," Gail whispered. "It wasn't a coincidence."

James pressed his lips together and closed his eyes. That wasn't possible. He and Charlie had shared a connection. She couldn't possibly have tricked him, could she?

"He must have made a mistake," James spoke in a low growl.

Gail put her hand on his arm. "Kyle doesn't make mistakes."

James looked around the car. Eric kept his eyes firmly on the road ahead and stayed out of the whole thing. Gail looked at James with big, apologetic eyes. Henry... well, he was just Henry. He was neither apologetic nor sensitive.

"She's been with the Edinburgh Herald for two years now," Henry said.

James didn't know what to think. In between the hurt and anger Charlie had shown yesterday, he had still seen the girl he used to know back in the day. He had seen it in her eyes; she still had feelings for him, despite everything. Could she be that good an actress?

For the rest of the drive, the discussion was over, though James could still feel Gail's eyes on him every so often. But there was nothing more to discuss.

Henry and Gail had made their point. James had to accept it.

He thought of everything they'd talked about. He'd shared some details about their activities, their reasons for going public. Had those very same details already made their way into today's papers? The Edinburgh Herald was a local rag, but news had a way of spreading.

Had he shared anything crucial? He wasn't sure anymore.

The car came to a halt in the same place it had done yesterday.

"I'll pick you guys up when I'm done with my meeting," Eric mumbled.

The three Scottish bears got out of the car in silence, and Eric drove off behind them. Then, James' pocket began to vibrate. He got his phone out. Charlie.

Henry and Gail exchanged a look, which he tried his best to ignore. He also ignored the call and put the phone back into his pocket.

"Let's go. We don't want to be late," James said.

Henry and Gail took the lead, and James followed. They passed through security and entered the building without incident. James was almost waiting for Charlie to show up again, intercepting them on their way to the Home Secretary's offices, but she was nowhere to be seen.

He wasn't sure how he'd react if he ran into her now. She'd lied to him by omission. She'd allowed him to think their reunion had been a coincidence. Still, he couldn't shake all those feelings he had towards her. It couldn't all have been an act from her side. Or was he so blinded by his own guilt and attraction that he just couldn't see the truth?

They were made to wait in a spacious wood paneled room, much nicer and more impressive than the one Eric's MP had received them in. The atmosphere was tense, and none of them spoke a word. Instead, James did his best to focus on the talking points they'd agreed on, while trying to forget about Charlie's deception.

About ten minutes later, the door behind them swung open, and the Home Secretary herself marched in, flanked by two armed guards. James was actually relieved to see the guards; finally, here was someone who had assessed the risks of meeting with three bear shifters and taken precautions.

"Morning," the Home Secretary said while scrutinizing each of the three visitors one by one. "What can I do for you?"

Despite the implied politeness of the question, James

knew that what she really meant was for the shifters to justify their presence here. So after a short introduction by Henry, James took over.

"Madam Secretary, essentially, some of our kind have appointed themselves as a sort of shadow government. They've created laws, which are being enforced by an agency I am sure you wouldn't want to associate with your government. Many of our kind have been made to believe that this shadow government is the only legitimate authority in our world, and whatever happens in London is irrelevant to us."

"This authority you speak of is the Alliance, which your group has grown out of, I suppose?" The woman folded her hands and kept her steely gaze locked on James. Considering how petite she was in comparison to the huge wooden desk, as well as the shifters opposite her, the Home Secretary still commanded immense respect. She had the body language of an alpha.

"That's right. Adrian Blacke - the Alliance's leader - is used to ruling his people the way he sees fit. Secrecy helped him secure his position, of course, now that we've forced his hand, he's scrambling to remain relevant in a post-reveal world. We believe he will approach you, if he hasn't already."

The woman nodded, and somehow still managed to give nothing away. She wasn't about to show her hand and share whether or not she'd already been in contact with Blacke, James thought. Of course, she wouldn't. Knowledge is power.

"The point is, Blacke is used to ruling with complete impunity. He has turned his own people against him - our organization and the support we've gained is evidence of that. Under his watch our struggle with a certain human element - who were aware of our secret before the reveal - has escalated as well," James explained.

"I see," she said.

"He will offer you access to certain schemes he's

planning to put in place to further oppress our people. His offer will seem tempting, the perfect way to control a segment of the population you didn't even know existed previously."

"And what do you offer?" she asked.

"Peaceful coexistence. Most of our kind are friendly, law-abiding people, who are just trying to make ends meet. We only rebel when backed into a corner. We just want our freedom."

"And what of the recent claims made that shifters have been killing people all over the country?" the Home Secretary asked.

James swallowed hard. Everyone in this room had skeletons in their closet from their work with Adrian Blacke's Alliance. If it all came out, they might have to face the music.

"The Sons of Domnall have been hunting our kind for generations. We have dossiers and evidence to back this up, which we would be happy to share. As long as we kept our existence a secret, we were left to our own devices to defend ourselves. You, Madam Secretary have a problem on your hands now. Our reveal has also exposed a vast terrorist network operating right under your nose. And we can help you dismantle it through the proper channels."

Gail and Henry exchanged a quick look next to James.

The Home Secretary remained silent, as though she was thinking over everything James had told her.

"It's simple, really. What would you like this government's - your - legacy to be? Freedom for all, or oppression and a potential genocide if the Sons of Domnall are left to run rampant?" James asked.

She nodded and pushed her chair back. "Alright. I have another appointment now, but I'd like to thank you for coming in today and sharing your concerns with me. Please leave your contact details with one of my aides so that my office may stay in touch to see all this to an acceptable conclusion."

James glanced at Gail and Henry, then back at the Home Secretary.

They all got up together, causing one of the guards to twitch slightly, though he didn't make a move. This was exactly the problem, James thought. The reveal had scared some people, and if they didn't handle the follow-up correctly, the Sons would be swamped with new recruits and supporters.

The Home Secretary nodded at each of the three bears individually and retreated through the same door, with both bodyguards at her side.

James breathed a sigh of relief.

"That went well," Gail remarked.

"I think so," James said.

"Let's wait, and see how it plays out first," Henry said. "We need to move forward with our media campaign as well. If public opinion sways our way, she'll have no choice but to work with us over Blacke or God forbid, the Sons."

Gail and James nodded. They needed to rally Jamie's family, and perhaps others who had seen tragedy at the hands of the Sons, or Blacke, or both, and quickly. And they needed a trustworthy reporter to cover the whole thing, ensuring that the story wasn't spun around to make them look bad.

James put his hand in his pocket instinctively. The only reporter he knew was Charlie. And she'd lied to him.

But did they have time to find someone else?

James followed Henry and Gail through the corridor, down the stairs and into the main lobby, where Charlie had found them yesterday. She was still nowhere to be seen. They left via the main door this time, only to be greeted by a large crowd of protesters.

There were hundreds of them. Some carried banners; some shouted slogans.

Animals belong in the zoo.

No monsters in my neighborhood.

A bear is always armed.

Along the front of the rally, a group of women stood in a line, each of them carrying a photograph of a different young man with the words *missing, presumed dead,* written underneath. James didn't dare look at any of them in case he recognized someone he'd seen in Blacke's dungeon.

The three bears kept their heads down as they passed by the crowd, hoping they wouldn't attract too much attention. The last thing they needed was to cause a scene.

"Call your friend," Henry said, as though he had read James' thoughts from before. "Figure out whose side she's on. Meanwhile, I'll call Jamie and Eric."

James nodded. Time was of the essence.

CHAPTER TEN

It was almost noon when Charlie's phone rang again.

Her chat with Ella had helped somewhat to calm her down, as had the cup of Chamomile tea she'd ordered to counter her anxiety. But the sound of her phone had startled her all over again.

This time, it *was* James.

Relief washed over her as she answered.

"Hey, James!" she said.

"Charlie," he sounded curt, putting her on edge again.

"What's wrong?"

"Nothing. Why would anything be wrong?" he said.

Charlie's heart started to beat faster. "I don't know. You sound... Anyway, what's up?" she stammered.

"I need to see you," James said.

That was exactly what she wanted as well, but now she was certain. Something was definitely wrong. She could hear it in his voice, and she'd already felt it all morning. If this was just paranoia, she was about to lose her mind.

"Okay... Where?" she asked.

"Marble Arch. Half an hour?"

"Sure. I'll be th-" the line had gone dead before Charlie had had the chance to finish her sentence. Had he just hung up on her? What the hell was going on?

Charlie packed up her things, paid for the tea and headed straight for the tube station down the road from her hotel. Half an hour to get to Marble Arch should be more than enough time. Still, she caught herself impatiently tapping her fingers on her shoulder bag as she waited for the next train to arrive. Time moved at a crawl, and the otherwise reasonable four-minute wait for her train felt endless.

Finally, it arrived, and she got on. It was overcrowded,

and she found herself stuck in the entrance area with no hope of getting a seat.

Still, she was glad to finally be making progress towards her destination. She had to get there on time and figure out what had happened with James to make him sound so tense. And of course, she had to clear the air between them. If she wanted a chance to move forward, there should be no more secrets.

A change and another crowded train later, she finally arrived at Marble Arch. Once Charlie made her way up to street level, she took a moment to find her bearings. It was impossible to miss the famous white landmark across the street.

There was no sign of James yet, so she waited. It was a clear winter's day, but the sun didn't do much to warm her. It had to be below freezing, and the coat that had kept her comfortable at the cafe had lost its efficacy. She hadn't even thought to keep a pair of gloves out.

"Charlie," a voice made her jump.

She turned, and there he was. James.

"Hi," she mumbled while rubbing her hands together and blowing into them in an attempt to warm up.

From one day to the next, his whole demeanor had changed. He'd gone from hot to icy cold.

"Tell me about your work at the Edinburgh Herald," he began.

Her heart sank, and her lower lip started to shake. So that's what this was. Just when she'd planned to tell him everything, he'd found out first. No wonder he was angry.

"That's exactly what I had wanted to talk to you about," she whispered.

His dark expression barely changed, and why would it? If she were in his position, any explanation she could offer now wouldn't convince her either.

"I should have told you yesterday," Charlie said while keeping her eyes fixed on the ground between them.

"I just need to know one thing," James began.

Charlie looked up but immediately averted her gaze again after making eye contact. As cold and angry as he sounded, he didn't look it. His eyes were filled with emotion, but there was no anger in them. He looked hurt more than anything else.

"What is it?" she asked.

"Did you submit anything yet?"

"What?" Charlie blurted out. "I would never! Sure, I used certain perks of the job to get out of the office and come here to see you. But I haven't reported back. In fact, after sabotaging my colleague's chances at a story by guiding you out the side entrance yesterday, I'm not even sure I still *have* a job."

Tears filled her eyes. How she regretted not telling him sooner. The more time she spent in his presence, or even thinking about him, the more she had started to wonder if perhaps they *could* give things a go again. It didn't make any sense, but now that everything hung in the balance, she knew exactly what she wanted. She wanted him back.

James sighed and looked around. "Walk with me," he said.

Charlie nodded and followed his lead. They walked across the small green patch around the Marble Arch in silence, crossed the road and entered Hyde Park.

"We have a proposal for you," James finally said.

We? So this was all business now? "Yeah?"

"You saw that protest on TV yesterday. We need to improve our image, so those *people* don't get the upper hand, you understand?"

Charlie didn't answer. This was exactly what she would have suggested, if only she'd had the chance to come clean about her work first.

"There was another protest yesterday outside Westminster," James added. "Knowing how they operate, they will escalate as soon as they've got the numbers they need. We'll all be targeted. We've been fighting these people for years, so we know they're capable of violence."

Charlie balled her fists in her pockets. This was bad. When Charlie had seen their leader's speech, she'd compared them to nationalists. And although nationalists did at times inspire hate crimes, they mainly sought a political solution to their problems: stricter immigration laws; closing the borders.

But this wasn't an immigration issue. Shifters already lived among them, and they seemed to be native to this place. How do you resolve a conflict with a native minority? The only examples history could offer painted a bleak picture.

"You think they want to instigate a genocide? Why would people even go along with that?" Charlie stammered. The thought seemed so preposterous when spoken out loud; she wasn't sure she wanted to believe it. And yet...

"You tell me. What's the logical next step?" James asked.

If people were scared enough... Anything was possible.

Charlie felt her chest tighten, which made her lose her balance slightly. She grabbed for James' arm to steady herself. "Oh my God," she whispered.

The second she touched him, she felt it again. The jolt of energy. The butterflies. The overwhelming urge to forget herself and get him back. This wasn't helpful. *Focus, woman!*

She let go and made a beeline for the nearest bench, where she sat down and rested her head in her hands. This was too much.

Tears were once again flowing freely.

This was ridiculous. She hadn't cried in years and now, in the span of three days, this was the third time!

James sat down beside her. She hadn't looked up and thus she hadn't seen him, but somehow she felt his presence right next to her. It made her cry even harder. She should have told him from the start. Instead, she ruined their second chance from the start.

It's okay... Please don't cry!

Charlie looked up and found James looking at her. His eyes seemed more intense than usual, as though they were glowing slightly. Had he just said that out loud? Had she just imagined it?

Please. I can't stand to see you cry.

There it was again! It wasn't like her to have such an active imagination.

How come I can hear you? Charlie thought.

The voice didn't respond. Instead, James took her hand in both of his. He was so warm; his touch sent shivers down her spine.

"I didn't mean to lie to you," Charlie said while looking down at her hand in between his. They were huge. Strong, and yet infinitely gentle.

How small she felt next to him. This was quite a feat; ever since she'd started to fill out a bit in college, she'd never had much cause to feel small or even vulnerable.

"I know," James said. "I know that you wanted to tell me."

How did he know?

I can feel it, the voice in her head said.

This whole thing, it was so unreal. Was she actually out here with him? Or would she wake up any moment now and find that it was all just a dream?

How is this possible?

Charlie looked up at him. His eyes had changed again. Gone was the pain she'd seen before. It had been replaced with the same tenderness and hope she'd seen yesterday.

This man was going to drive her crazy with his mood swings.

"We may have shown ourselves to the world now, but there's still a lot you need to know about our kind," he said.

"I've got time," Charlie whispered.

Neither of them broke eye contact. The air between them seemed to be heavy with tension.

"Well," James started. "When a man meets a woman... and they really like each other." He winked at her.

"Don't tell me you're going to talk about birds and bees next," Charlie remarked.

"There she is, my old friend Charlie McAllister. She's back!" James joked.

Charlie scoffed but couldn't suppress a smile.

"So I was saying. When a couple *really* like each other, they connect on a deeper level."

James' tone was serious again. No matter how strange it sounded, he was no longer joking.

"And then they hear voices?" Charlie asked.

"They can communicate by thought, yes."

Charlie shook her head. If she hadn't just experienced it, she would have never believed it.

"You're a weird lot; you know that?" she said.

James shrugged. "There are a lot of upsides. If you can deal with crazy paranoid humans hunting you."

"Such as?"

"Well, couples have no secrets. They're faithful for life. When a shifter finds their true mate, they become whole together."

"But I'm not a shifter," Charlie remarked.

"I know. And that's why I left back then. Under the old rules, we were only supposed to pair up within our species. But I've since learned that it works the same even if one partner is human."

"Wait, are you trying to tell me that simply because I kissed a shifter when I was seventeen, I basically ruined any hope of ever having a relationship with anyone else? And if we hadn't run into one another now, I would have remained single forever?" Charlie asked.

"Uhh..." James looked away sheepishly. "If it helps, there's been no one else in my life either."

Charlie sat back on the bench and looked across the open views of the park ahead of them. "That's so weird."

James put his arm around her, causing her to close her

eyes involuntarily. Who could have guessed that today would turn out this way? Sure, she'd hoped it would, but when he confronted her about her work, she had lost all hope.

"James Finch?" a voice interrupted them. A man approached. His hair was cropped short, and he was wearing a black leather biker jacket, jeans, and heavy black boots.

Charlie could feel James tense up beside her. Although there was nothing obviously wrong yet, she sensed the danger his instincts had alerted him to. This telepathic communication thing really did work.

"Who wants to know?" James asked.

"Victor Domnall sends his regards," the man said.

Knife! Within a split second, James pushed her down the bench and flung himself at the stranger in a blur of claws and fur. That's when the darkness claimed Charlie.

CHAPTER ELEVEN

By the time James got Charlie back to Eric's place, everyone was on high alert. She was still out, so he laid her down on his bed before joining the rest of the crew in the living area.

Everyone sat around, lost in thought, but Henry was furious.

"How could this happen?" he demanded. "Were you followed?"

James thought back to earlier that day. He'd been upset after finding out about Charlie's job. Had he let his guard down? It was possible.

"I'm not sure. I sure as hell didn't see anyone," James said. Then again, he had been so focused on Charlie, he hadn't even seen the guy videoing the whole thing on his phone.

"And did you *have* to charge at him the way you did? It's all over Facebook now!" Henry paced back and forth.

"He tried to attack my mate with a knife. What would you have done?" James felt himself get angry all over again. Of all people, Henry should understand. He would stop at nothing to defend Gail.

"Oh. She's your *mate* now, is she?" Henry barked.

James stood tall and faced his leader, staring him down with only inches between them. "Yes, she is. What are you going to do about it?"

"Now, now. Let's all relax," Gail spoke up from the sofa. "We can't change what happened. And if Charlotte is James' mate, so be it. The freedom to pair up with whoever you like is one of the fundamental reasons the

New Alliance came into existence."

Henry backed down and joined Gail, though his expression still betrayed his displeasure. James retreated as well. Henry was right, though. This was bad. The Sons could spin this any way they wanted.

"We need to do some damage control before this hits the evening news," Gail said. "Sure, the police arrested the attacker and let James go, so that's a good sign. But that in itself might not be convincing enough."

James nodded, as did Henry and Eric, who had so far stayed out of the whole conversation.

"Once she wakes up... And if she indeed is your mate," Henry's skeptical tone grated at James, but he decided to let it go for now. "Perhaps she can help us."

James shook his head. "No way. They've seen her face now and already tried to attack her once. I'm not going to let you make a bigger target out of her."

Henry glared at James. "What choice do we have? We need friends in the media now more than ever. We already agreed on that."

"Yeah, we agreed. But things have changed," James growled.

"Bull-" Henry started, but then glanced over at Gail and stopped talking.

"Guys, if you'll allow me to say something," Gail took over. "She works for a morning newspaper, yes? We need to fix this now, today. If she knows someone else who can help..."

"Wait, you said it's all over Facebook. Can't Kyle help somehow? Hack in and remove the video?" James suggested.

"I'll ask... But we still have to manage the fallout; we need a plan," Henry said.

James nodded. As much as he hated to admit it, Henry

was right.

"He knew my name. How did he know my name?" James wondered aloud.

Gail shrugged. "Maybe they have their own computer guy. Your face has been all over the news since we came out. With the right know-how, I'm sure it's not that hard to find out someone's identity. Kyle probably could have done it."

She made sense, but James still felt there was something more to it. In his years working for Blacke, his intuition hadn't failed him even once. He hardly dared to consider the consequences if somehow the Sons had gained support within law enforcement. If that were the case, then everyone in this room would have to look over their shoulders from now on.

"Talk to her," Henry repeated himself. "We need to sort this out as soon as possible."

James wanted to argue for Charlie's safety again but didn't get the chance.

"No need," a female voice interrupted their conversation.

James closed his eyes as she approached. Her presence overwhelmed him now, so strong was their connection; their attraction. No matter what happened, what she'd kept from him before, it was impossible to ignore or fight her pull. They belonged together, for better or for worse.

"I'm in. Just tell me what you need me to do," Charlie spoke directly to Henry now.

———— ◆ ————

When Charlie woke up, she barely remembered the confusing events at the park. She blinked a few times in an attempt to let her eyes adjust to the darkness of the strange room she found herself in. Slowly, outlines of furniture came into view. She was in a single bed, still fully dressed. The side of her head was tender, as though she'd been bruised somehow. Across from her bed, stood another one with a desk and chair in between underneath the window. Where was she?

She closed her eyes again and inhaled deeply. James had been here. His scent lingered on the pillow, which reassured her. She was safe.

After laying there, finding her bearings for another minute or two, she got up to investigate the rest of the house. She opened the door and heard voices coming from down the hall. One she recognized as James, the other, she wasn't sure. They were arguing.

As she walked along the hallway, the cold of the tiles underfoot alerted her to the fact that she wasn't wearing her shoes anymore. Still, she didn't just march into what she presumed was the living room. No, she stayed back a bit and listened. Something about a video on Facebook. They needed help to manage the fallout from it.

This tied in perfectly with the idea she'd had at night. She could help these guys swing public opinion their way. She could help appeal to people's hearts to convince them the shifters weren't the bad guys here.

"Talk to her. We need to sort this out as soon as possible," one of the men - the one she'd heard arguing with James before - said.

That was her cue.

"No need. I'm in," Charlie spoke as she stepped into the room that contained about a half dozen shifters, mostly men. All eyes were on her all of a sudden. "Just tell me what you need me to do."

She glanced over at James, who was staring at her as well now. She could feel him so keenly now; it was unnerving. If this was what it meant to be part of a couple, she had to wonder how these people got any work done whatsoever.

Charlie closed her eyes and took a deep breath, and she sat down on the couch beside James, taking his hand. *It'll be fine. Let me help.*

"Very well," the man across from them said. Charlie recognized him as the one who had been there with James at the House of Commons the day before. "Take a look at this."

He got up and handed her a phone; on it was a video of what had happened at the park. Her memories had been sketchy, but even so, the video wasn't much better. Everything had happened so fast that the camera had had trouble capturing it all. Within a couple of minutes, it was over.

"This sort of reminds me of those ambiguous bigfoot or yeti videos - no offense," Charlie spoke. "It's not very clear."

"None taken," the woman who'd been with James yesterday as well spoke with a subtle smile playing on her lips.

That's Gail, and the man next to her is Henry. They're a couple, Charlie heard James' voice in her head. Very convenient indeed, being able to communicate like this without anyone else knowing.

"Here's the deal. I work at a paper up in Edinburgh, but I'm not high up or anything. If you want to influence how this is perceived, I'm going to have to convince my boss to help us."

"Is he trustworthy?" Henry asked.

"If we offer him an exclusive of some sort, I don't see how he could refuse."

Henry and Gail nodded, as did most of the other

people she'd never met before.

"Very well, so here's the deal," Henry started. He explained the back story of Matthew Brown's childhood kidnapping many years ago by a rogue Sons member, and how he'd only recently been reunited with his family. He spoke of Jamie, a member of the Edinburgh Alliance, who had paired up with a prominent Sons member's daughter who had switched sides. All of these people would be willing to face the media to make their case against the Sons of Domnall.

Charlie noticed her bag leaning against the side of one of the sofas and got her notepad out. She wrote down everything Henry told her, as well as her own ideas for how to best present the story. By the end of it, she'd filled three A4 sized pages.

"This all sounds promising. My boss will salivate over it; I can guarantee it," she said. "If that's all, I should make the call."

James squeezed her hand. *Are you sure you want to do this?*

Charlie smiled briefly. *Anything, as long as it helps keep you guys safe.*

So it was agreed. Charlie got up, grabbed her phone and notepad and retreated to the bedroom she'd just woken up in. Penderton would give her an earful, at least at first. But this was necessary. James had charged at the guy at the park without hesitation, and in the process potentially ruined the shifters' image. The least she could do was call up Penderton. What was he going to do? Yell? Fire her? Once he heard her story, he *had* to come around.

She dialed his number with trembling fingers and waited. The phone rang once, twice...

"McAllister, what a surprise!" His tone was heavy with sarcasm. "I thought you'd vanished permanently."

"Sir, please hear me out. That lead I told you about the

other day? It panned out. I managed to track them down, and I'm on the inside with the New Alliance."

"Wait... what? You were supposed to talk to someone who *knew* them! Instead, you fall off the radar for two days. Who knows if these people are who they say they are. And if you're talking to the actual New Alliance, I need an experienced reporter on the story, not you!" he argued.

The experienced reporter rant again. Charlie took a deep breath to maintain her cool.

"Sir, if you could please log on to Facebook. See the trending topics. At the top, there's a video which I'm sure will prove that I'm telling the truth."

Penderton didn't say a word; there was only rustling on the other end of the line. Then she could hear the beginning of the video when the stranger called out James' name. Penderton let out a slow whistle, presumably when Charlie came into view.

"Okay, McAllister. I'm listening," he finally said.

Charlie felt a rush of excitement as she picked up her notepad. This was her chance!

She went through the whole story Henry had told her. About the disappearance of little Matthew Brown, the desertion of Alison Campbell from the Sons of Domnall, as well as her role in the capture of her father.

Penderton barely said a word, though she could hear him scribbling it all down at his end as well.

Charlie ended on the most important point of all: that if he wanted exclusive access to these prominent New Alliance members, he had to figure out a way to spin this video in their favor, and do it fast. The exclusive interviews and other content would keep flowing, as long as Penderton guaranteed it made the New Alliance look good. It was mutually beneficial cooperation they were after, and they wouldn't approach any other media outlets as long as Penderton and the Edinburgh Herald remained their allies.

"Understood. I'll get things moving immediately," Penderton said. "And... McAllister, good work." Charlie forgot to breathe as she heard these words.

Finally. The recognition she deserved.

CHAPTER TWELVE

Once she'd finished her call with Penderton, Charlie breathed a big sigh of relief. No matter the twists or turns in this story, she had achieved what she'd set out to do. And in the end, she didn't even need to deceive anyone either.

She lay the phone down on the bed and stared at its black screen for a moment. Penderton was on it, and knowing how he worked, he'd get some kind of strategy together quickly.

Only now did Charlie realize how exhausted she still was. The events at the park had taken a toll on her. The bruise on her head throbbed. She hadn't even checked herself out in the mirror yet; who knew how bad it looked?

The door opened behind her, and it seemed the atmosphere of the room instantly changed. She didn't even need to turn to see who it was, because she already knew. James.

He rested his hands on her shoulders and started to massage her.

You're tired. You should rest.

Charlie closed her eyes. His touch was magic.

I promised to help, so that's what I need to do. She put her hand on his. It didn't make sense, how much she wanted him. How absolutely desperate she was for his affection now. Gone were the doubts and anger she'd felt when they had lunch together. Even the memories of the heartache he'd caused had faded.

She'd never felt this way, except perhaps during that one moment they'd shared so long ago.

Funny, she'd never even believed in true love or any of that stuff. Some people - Ella most notably - were quick to call her a cynic, but Charlie considered herself a realist.

Not anymore.

She believed now.

Charlie turned to face James and found that his eyes were that same funny color again like at the park. They definitely *were* glowing now.

You're the most beautiful woman I've ever seen.

Charlie pressed her lips together and averted her gaze. Nobody had ever told her that.

You're not so bad yourself, she thought, as she looked up at him again. Bloody hell, he was gorgeous.

"Why are all shifters so handsome?" she wondered aloud.

James chuckled. "They're not. Shifters all look the same. Humans are beautiful in their diversity."

Charlie frowned. She'd never thought of it like that.

James sat down in front of her on the bed and raised his hand to her cheek.

I want to kiss you again.

He leaned forward, his face neared hers until their lips were just a fraction of an inch apart.

His scent intoxicated her, making her feel faint. She reached out for his upper arm to steady herself.

Then, the intrusive ring of her phone made her flinch. James pulled back and held it up to her. "I guess that's your boss?"

Yep, it was Penderton all right.

Charlie sighed. "The man isn't known for his timing."

James smiled and let his gaze linger on her lips. "You'd better get it before he changes his mind about helping us."

"True," Charlie said and raised the phone to her ear. "Mr. Penderton."

"McAllister, here's what we will do: I've made a few calls and set up a press conference for four o'clock. All the major news outlets are sending someone."

Charlie checked her watch. Not much time to go on. She had known he was well connected, but even so, everything was happening very quickly indeed.

"Okay, and then?" Charlie picked up a pen, readying herself to take notes.

"Start the press conference by playing the video. It's already out there, and you can't deny it. All you can do now is attempt to control the narrative. Point out the threat posed by the attacker. How this is typical of the kind of persecution shifters have had to endure at the hands of the Sons of Domnall. Get some photos up of victims already claimed by the struggle. Focus on the protective nature of shifters, how they'd sacrifice themselves to keep their loved ones happy. Make the public love them."

"Wait... you mean for *me* to attend the press conference?" Charlie dropped her pen in disbelief.

"Why, yes of course! If they speak for themselves, it'll be less convincing. Plus, you're in the video, so you might as well own it. Once you've said your piece, let one of the New Alliance take over and confirm the message. The people have nothing to fear unless they attack first."

James took Charlie's hand and squeezed it gently.

It's too dangerous. Let someone else handle it, his voice urged.

She shook her head. Penderton was right. And she was already in the video anyway.

"I understand." *I have to, James. I have to do this.* She picked up the pen again.

"That's step one. Step two; talkshow appearances for those people you mentioned. The brothers who have only recently been reunited and the rest of their family. The public will lap up their story. They'll do the morning show circuit; regional as well as national. We'll keep hammering the viewing public with their story until *everyone* knows it by heart. We want to get people talking about it at work, at school, everywhere. This will take some time to set up, of course, in the meanwhile, have them call me, and I'll see to it that they receive some media training. At the same time, we'll get missing persons spots on the reality crime shows. Those features will subconsciously teach the public that a lot of shifters have been harmed by the Sons; that shifters are the victims here."

"Okay..." Charlie struggled to write fast enough. In truth, her mind was somewhere else already. Penderton meant for her to be the New Alliance's spokesperson. She'd never been on TV, though, of course, her journalism degree had covered the basics of every type of media, so she'd done some role playing. But that was a few years ago now...

"McAllister. Are you listening?" Penderton demanded.

"I'm sorry. I was just thinking."

"You'll be fine. Get to the Grosvenor by three-thirty."

"Wait, the conference is at the Grosvenor?" *How on earth did he swing that?*

"The manager owes me a favor. Don't worry about that. Just get there, understood?"

"Yes, Sir."

"Good," Penderton said, and the line went dead.

Charlie couldn't believe what had just happened.

"Oh my God," she stammered, as she put her phone down on the bed between James and her. She looked up at him and found that he was already staring at her. The concern in his eyes was clear as day. But at least he didn't argue for her to change her mind anymore. She'd made her choice, so he would accept it.

She glanced down at her notes again. Press conference. Talk shows. Her head swam.

"I'll go tell Henry the plan. And that Jamie, Alison and Matthew are to contact your boss." James suggested. *We'll pick up where we left off after the conference.* He winked at her, making her smile despite herself. He got up and left her to prepare.

Charlie blinked a few times to get the notes back into focus again.

They didn't have much time, and she needed to know exactly what she was going to say. The last thing they needed was a newbie journalist fumbling over her words. That would ruin any chance they had to get the public on their side.

But most of all, she needed a paracetamol. Luckily she always had some in her bag. *Did shifters take medicines like humans did?* She'd make sure to ask James later.

———— ♦ ————

When Charlie arrived in the marble-clad lobby of the Grosvenor hotel with James, Henry, and Gail, they were greeted by the last person she expected to see.

"McAllister. So it's true," Diane Goodwin said.

The two rivals eyed each other suspiciously.

"Diane." Of course. She'd been in town chasing the same story already, so it was obvious Penderton would rope her in to help set up the event.

"The stage is ready," Diane nodded in the direction of one of the conference rooms. "People will start to arrive soon. We'll play the video, I'll introduce everyone, and then you take over."

Charlie swallowed hard. "Yeah. That's fine."

James placed his hand on her shoulder, which did help in giving her some strength. Of course, Diane noticed the gesture instantly as well and rolled her eyes.

"If you need make-up, someone's waiting for you behind the stage," she said.

Charlie waited as Henry and Gail made their way to the conference room already.

Diane leaned forward a bit, perhaps hoping to stay out of James' earshot - an impossibility, as long as they were in the same room.

"One of these days, you'll have to let me know how you managed all this," Diane said.

Charlie shrugged. "Just lucky, I guess."

"Yeah..." Diane glanced at James and back at Charlie. "Well, you best get yourself ready. I'm going to make sure everyone finds their way inside."

James placed his arm around Charlie's shoulder, and

they both walked into the conference room. Bloody hell. Was she really going to sit up there in just a short while? In front of the stage stood at least fifty empty chairs. Surely they weren't expecting *that* many reporters? Not at such short notice?

Charlie inhaled sharply and breathed out slowly, like how they'd taught her during her course. *Relax. It'll be fine.*

She sat down behind the stage and closed her eyes while the makeup artist Diane had arranged got to work. There wasn't much to be done. Just bare minimum touch-ups so she would come across well on TV.

You can do this, James encouraged her.

She smiled. Normally if someone said something like that to her, she might have brushed it away as just politeness. But with James she didn't just hear his words but felt his true intentions and feelings as well. He meant it.

With her hair and makeup done, Charlie got up and started to pace around while rehearsing her speech in her head. Walking always did help calm her down. As did the breathing exercises from her course. But most of all, it was James' support that kept her from freaking out.

Before she knew it, it was time. She signaled at Henry and Gail to join her; obviously, James had never left her side. The four of them climbed up onto the stage and took their seats. The formerly empty chairs in front of the podium had mostly filled up. The turnout was amazing.

Charlie squeezed James' hand underneath the table and scanned the crowd. This was major.

All the big networks seemed to be represented here. Charlie thought she recognized some of the faces in the crowd.

The lights turned on, and Diane marched up on stage, carrying a microphone.

"Esteemed members of the press, welcome! And thank you so much for joining us today." Diane spoke with so much ease, it was impossible for Charlie to suppress the sting of jealousy. She closed her eyes as Diane introduced them and the topic for the press conference. Breathe in sharply, exhale slowly... Breathe in, breathe out...

She opened her eyes just in time to catch the video on the large screen beside them in her peripheral vision.

You can do this, James encouraged her.

The video finished, and Charlie's heartbeat surged in a crescendo of nerves and determination as she adjusted the microphone in front of her. "Thank you, Diane." Charlie nodded in her colleague's direction. "Hello everyone, and welcome. I want you to know that I am one of you." Charlie took a deep breath and channeled all her energy into remembering her lines. "But I have been lucky to get to know the members of the New Alliance over the last few days. I have learned of the challenges they've faced. And the great love and companionship they're capable of." Charlie's voice grew more steady with each word. "Today, an unfortunate incident happened, which you've just seen in the video. We were publicly attacked, for no reason other than James being different."

Every sentence Charlie spoke was interrupted by camera flashes, but she kept on going just like she'd rehearsed.

"Today was different, in the sense that the incident was captured on camera for all to see. But these sort of hate crimes have been happening for years. The organization led by Victor Domnall has been targeting shifters since before they made their presence known to the world. You'd be hard pressed to find a shifter who doesn't know of someone hurt or lost in this struggle."

Charlie glanced over at James, who seemed to not even notice all the cameras and eager faces in front of them; he only had eyes for her. "Yet they haven't lost hope. They haven't lost the faith that if given the chance, humanity will accept and perhaps even embrace them. They're not after a fight; they just want to get by like the rest of us."

Charlie smiled briefly. James was right. Everything was

going to be fine. As she continued through the rest of her part of the conference, her confidence kept growing. She might never have set out to become the New Alliance's spokesperson, but now that she had started on this path, it felt right. This way she could do her bit to help them. Their faces were already out there. They were already targets unless they could get the public on their side. This was the right way forward - the only way forward.

CHAPTER THIRTEEN

James had hardly been able to take his eyes off Charlie throughout the conference. He'd been confident that she'd do well, even when she felt doubtful herself. But in the end, she blew him away along with the rest of the crowd.

When Henry took over and introduced himself as leader of the New Alliance for the audience questions segment of the conference, James grabbed Charlie's hand again. Although he wanted nothing more than to just look at her some more, he now kept an eye on the audience instead.

Their body language, combined with the sort of questions being asked gave him a reading of the mood in the room. These reporters acted very different than the ones they'd first revealed themselves to. Gone was the shock, the fear.

Perhaps it was because there were so many of them faced with only three shifters this time? Or it was a sign that their efforts to educate were starting to make an impact.

Charlie, of course, had been very sympathetic, whereas Henry wasn't really. He remained professional and kept a certain distance between himself and the audience. And that was fine; he was their leader, after all. That is why they'd agreed that for particularly sensitive questions, Gail would be the one to answer.

The questions lasted for another half hour. Most of them aimed at Henry, Gail, and even Charlie. Though a few to do directly with the attack were for James himself. Still, he couldn't wait to get out of there.

The moment everything was over, and the four of them got up and off the stage, James' focus had completely shifted. *Charlie.* She glanced over at him, a subtle smile playing on her lips. She knew exactly what was going on in his head.

"Eric will have recorded the live coverage. Let's go back and review it," Gail suggested.

James took Charlie's hand. How small and delicate her fingers were. He would never tire of how her presence made him feel. And to think how close they came to being forced apart again. This deep connection, the one shifters and their true mates shared had helped them overcome it all.

"Actually, I hope you don't mind if we catch up with you tomorrow. Charlie has been through a lot today; a bit of rest would do her good," James said.

You don't mind, do you? he thought.

Couldn't have said it better myself, she replied.

Gail and Henry exchanged a look.

"Fine. I suppose there's nothing more to be done today anyway," Henry said.

Where's your hotel? James asked.

Charlie squeezed his hand. *I thought you said I should rest.*

Of course... eventually.

As if on cue, Charlie's phone rang.

Penderton, she thought. She excused herself and walked off to the other end of the stage to answer.

"I think it went quite well," Gail said.

James nodded. "Couldn't have gone better."

Their small talk was interrupted by Charlie's colleague, who had taken the stage to introduce them at the start of the conference.

"Hello, I'm Diane. Nice to meet all of you," she smiled politely but hesitated before finally offering her hand.

"Good work, Diane," Henry said.

"Thanks..." she glanced back at the dark stage. Was she nervous?

Now that James had had a taste of what it was like to read someone's mind, he wished that talent extended to more than just one person. Unfortunately, that wasn't how it worked.

"You might want to take the back exit if you want to avoid the crowd..." Diane suggested.

Henry nodded and placed his arm on Gail's shoulder. James watched as the two of them followed Diane out of the conference room. Funny, how fate worked. James had always felt they were a rather odd match.

His idle observations were interrupted by Charlie, who returned with her phone still in her hand. The moment she got close, James' entire being seemed to respond. His bear was raring to break free and take what was his.

"That was Penderton," she explained.

"I know," James responded. "What did he say?"

"He was watching. Thought it went very well."

"That it did. You were amazing," James said.

Charlie grinned at him. "You're just biased."

"That may be. Doesn't make it less true." James smiled back at her.

Those full lips. How he yearned to feel them against his again. They'd been interrupted before, but he wouldn't let that happen this time.

Charlie had been the first and only girl to ever catch his eye. The years they'd spent apart had done nothing to change that. If anything, she was even more beautiful, more desirable now.

Stop thinking like that, or I'll give in to temptation right here, and we might have a shifter sex scandal on our hands, Charlie teased.

She was still the same old Charlie, with whom nothing was off limits. James knew she was only half joking, though. He felt her desire as though it were his own.

So let's get out of here.

He grabbed her hand and took the lead. Out the same double doors which Diane had shown Henry and Gail out from only minutes earlier. Diane's perfume hung in the air, making it easy for James to follow her route. They rushed outside, avoiding the reporters who would have lingered around the main lobby still.

James put his arm around Charlie's shoulder. In good old British fashion, the weather had turned during the two hours they'd spent inside for the conference. An icy cold drizzle was falling now as clouds shrouded the city, obscuring much of the skyline.

"Where to, madam spokesperson?" James joked.

Charlie took out her phone for directions. "This way," she said, pointing up at the road ahead.

He wrapped his arm tighter around her, aiming to protect her from the elements as best he could and off they went.

***

Charlie wasn't sure what exactly had happened through most of the press conference. Equally, she had no idea how she'd found her way back to her hotel.

But here they were.

She looked at James, who was taking off his coat and hanging it over a chair to dry. Charlie followed his example.

Was this actually happening? The culmination of all those forbidden teenage fantasies was finally coming true?

Her sensible side should have doubts. She should wonder about why she could trust him to stay now after he'd just left the last time. She should equally worry about whether they were even compatible at all. Different species, different backgrounds. She should be concerned about what this meant for the future. Did this mean they could never have a family? Who knew how compatible their biology would be?

But her head wasn't doing much thinking right now; her heart was. And that was convinced that somehow, everything was going to be all right.

James stepped up to her, cupping her face in his hands. She didn't want to wait anymore. This time, nobody and nothing could interrupt them.

She tiptoed to get closer to his level and wrapped her

arms around his neck. His scent filled her nostrils. Like a classy aftershave, only better. The anticipation threatened to overwhelm.

Charlie closed her eyes and felt herself become weightless in his arms.

Finally, their lips touched, releasing a decade of tension and frustrations. So soft, his lips were. So gentle.

He tasted even better than she remembered.

Words couldn't describe the feeling of the tips of their tongues dancing around each other. Butterflies? Certainly not. Fireworks? Not even close.

It was as though her whole body was on fire, and the only thing to soothe the burn was him. His kisses, his touch.

Charlie opened her eyes and was instantly mesmerized by the raging inferno in his.

James carried her over to the bed and laid her down gently on her back. She refused to let go of him, forcing him to climb on top of her.

Their hands, now hungry to catch up on lost time, roamed the other's bodies. Discovering, familiarizing, conquering whatever was in reach. She tore at his shirt, which finally gave way at the seams. Meanwhile, he took her blouse in his teeth and ripped all the buttons right off it in one swift tug.

There she lay on her back, exposed. How different their bodies were. Soft curves against hard muscle. Charlie thought again about what he'd said. How shifters were all the same and humans were more beautiful because they were different. It made sense the other way around too.

The body that rested on top of her was uniquely beautiful; a human lover would have been different. Not so strong, so tall, definitely not that muscular. This was a level of perfection you didn't normally find out in the real world.

He dove down and tasted her skin. Nibbling, sucking and licking at her cleavage; leaving sweet pleasure wherever his mouth went.

She couldn't do much more except enjoy herself. She was helplessly at his mercy.

With one hand, he rid her of her bra, giving him even more exposed skin to play with.

Charlie grabbed for his hair, tugging at it playfully at first. But when his lips found her nipple, she lost almost all control.

The rougher she touched him, the more turned on he seemed to get. Still, he took care not to hurt her. Their levels of strength were so vastly different, and yet he knew exactly how to touch her right.

After teasing her nipples, one after the other, he slid down further and sucked on her belly button and nibbled on the skin surrounding it. Charlie wouldn't have expected it to earlier, but even that felt good.

Then, he raised himself off her and looked into her eyes.

"I want to go down on you," he said in a low growl.

It wasn't a question but a demand. Not that Charlie had the self-control or desire to say no anyway.

She bit her lip and looked him over top to bottom. The look in his eyes gave her chills, but in a good way. And that flawless body, was all that really hers to enjoy now?

He was still wearing his jeans, but she'd make sure that wouldn't be the case for long. In the meantime, though, she wiggled out of her skirt and finally her tights and panties.

James didn't waste any time. The moment she was fully nude, he spread her legs apart and dove right in for his first taste of her.

Charlie moaned and clawed at the sheets, so intense was the pleasure he dished out. She closed her eyes, as he licked her deeply, then took her clit in between his lips. He repeated that same move again and again, edging her further towards ecstasy each time.

How was it that he knew exactly what to do? She

couldn't have told him this. She had no way of knowing how good this would feel.

And yet...

He pushed his tongue into her again, causing her to buck up her hips at him. She had precious little control over herself.

"Oh God!" she cried out.

She had nothing to compare this to, except the occasional illicit dreams she'd had of him over the years. Was it always this good? Something told her that it wasn't; what they shared right now was something special, which most people would never experience.

He got up on one elbow while licking at her clit again. Charlie writhed against the sheets with pleasure. Then he touched her, running the tip of his finger along her folds, and made her cry out all over again.

He inserted one, then two fingers, all the while continuing to lick at her most sensitive spot. *More! Deeper!*

Charlie was done for. As he circled his finger over her G-spot, she lost the last shred of control. Her orgasm overwhelmed her before she had a chance to realize what was happening. She cried out his name, her whole body quivering with the aftershocks of her release.

Then, just like that, his two fingers were gone, as was his mouth.

Charlie opened her eyes to beg him for more, when she caught a glimpse of him casting off his jeans. Before she could say a word, he was back on top of her, filling the void his fingers had left with his cock.

Bloody hell, Charlie thought. *How are you so good at this?*

James didn't respond, just looked down at her. From her eyes, his gaze traveled downward to her lips. Charlie wrapped her arms around him and drew him closer.

His rhythm sped up; the slow, careful first movements made way for more urgent, feverish thrusts. It wasn't just her on the brink of pleasure anymore. He was right there with her.

She wrapped her legs around his waist and closed her eyes again.

The strange thing was, she could still see him above her. And she could feel his pleasure, as he did hers.

Faster and faster he thrust into her. Charlie dug her nails into his back, which only seemed to encourage him further.

She started to moan, louder and louder. He pressed his lips against her, muffling her cries. Charlie was on the brink again, when he slipped his hands between the mattress and her back and lifted her up against him. He didn't miss a single beat; going faster, harder, deeper, while she clung on to him, unable and unwilling to let go.

She first felt it in her lower abdomen; a certain tension, which grew until it seemed to fill her chest too. His final push was like a pin prick to a balloon. As his cock pulsated and twitched inside of her, all that pleasure was released, causing it to travel through her whole body. From her abdomen out, reaching even the tips of her fingers, and the soles of her feet. She could keenly feel every nerve, every inch of her skin, as her body celebrated their union.

They stayed like that for minutes, perhaps hours, Charlie couldn't tell anymore. Their bodies entwined and connected, as one.

Charlie blinked a few times until his face came into focus again. There was nothing to say, nothing more to be done. His eyes seemed to smile at her, and she smiled back.

They had come a long way since that first, awkward kiss ten years ago.

Now she knew they were meant to be. There was no turning back, no chance of changing their minds.

Everything was going to be all right.

James had always been the one for her. The one she loved, even when she thought he didn't love her back. And even though he hadn't said it yet, she knew she'd been wrong.

He'd always loved her too.

EPILOGUE

"Welcome back," the Home Secretary spoke as she entered the room, flanked by two armed guards.

Charlie took a deep breath and got up to greet her along with the rest of them; James, Henry, and Gail.

"Please, take a seat," the woman said as she sat down behind her large mahogany desk. "We have a lot to discuss."

Charlie opened a fresh page in her notepad and started to write. This was her first big job covering a New Alliance story for Penderton, and she wasn't going to miss a thing.

"Thank you for meeting us again," Henry said.

His forced tone amused Charlie, who had learned in the time she'd known him that pleasantries were not part of his usual vocabulary. This was all Gail, working behind the scenes.

"Firstly, we're working on drawing up some amendments to existing legislation which will include shifters at an equal footing with humans. Any rights and duties enjoyed by the citizens of this country will extend equally to your people." The Home Secretary folded her hands and looked directly at each of her visitors. "Of course, this process will take some time, so I ask for your patience in letting the government follow its usual processes."

"Of course," Henry said. "We are pleased to hear of these positive developments."

Charlie scribbled it all down, along with a note to get her colleague Diane to find out which exact laws were going to be amended, and what the implications would be. Governance and politics were her specialty after all.

"Next, Victor Domnall is still in the wind. Ever since that press conference of yours-" The woman put on some reading glasses and adjusted them until they sat on the tip of her nose. "Scotland Yard has been picking up a lot of chatter, but they don't seem ready to act yet. The winds are changing, and the effects are starting to be felt."

Charlie smiled subtly. She could feel James smiling beside her too, which still amazed her. Ever since their first night together - and of course, every other night since then - she'd been able to sense him so much more clearly. She could almost see him if he was nearby, without looking at him. She could feel his presence and hear his thoughts through walls now.

"As long as they're still out there, they pose a threat," Henry said.

Charlie flinched and started to write again. *Focus!*

"Agreed. They've gone unchecked for too long. Sure, you've had your own initiative in place against them, but that's no longer an option."

Henry leaned forward as though he wanted to argue but must have changed his mind at the last moment. He remained quiet for now.

"If your goal is to coexist in human society, it's imperative that you follow human laws. We don't tolerate vigilantism. A crime is a crime, no matter who commits it, or who the victim is." The Home Secretary stared Henry straight in the face now. She wasn't messing around.

Charlie was secretly glad she was only here to observe.

"If our people are in danger, something must be done, though. We must have some recourse," Henry said. His voice, as well as his body language, were tense now.

"I'm coming to that. But first I want your assurance

that your people aren't going to go off and take things into their own hands anymore. We can't accept such behavior as part of a civilized society. We don't go around kidnapping and hurting those who disagree with us."

The Home Secretary's tone, combined with those glasses balancing on her nose reminded Charlie of their old headmistress back home.

She looks an awful lot like Mrs. Bunnings, Charlie thought.

Stop it. You're going to make me laugh, James responded.

Charlie kept her head down and continued to take notes of the back and forth between Henry and the Home Secretary. In the end, Henry conceded, but his agreement was dependent on the safety of his people.

Charlie wondered how the others would take this. In the past weeks, she'd heard the story of Matthew Brown's abduction so many times she could recite it by heart. But that wasn't the only tragedy orchestrated by the Sons of Domnall. In Jamie's crew in Edinburgh, there was a guy named Aidan McMillan, whose parents had been killed by the Sons. In every city, every New Alliance splinter group, there were people who had been affected in this struggle. So much pain and heartache would be difficult to overcome.

"That's fair. We will set up an initiative to ensure shifters can live freely, and safely, within our borders." The Home Secretary picked up a dossier from her desk and handed it to Henry, who opened it. "Here is a proposal put together by various agencies. There will be a joint task force. Part human, part shifter. It'll be run independently but work closely with local law enforcement, even Interpol. This task force will follow the normal protocols as far as they're relevant and report directly to me."

Charlie looked at Henry to gauge his reaction. He was impossible to read. Gail, however, seemed pleasantly surprised as she grabbed Henry's arm.

That's good, isn't it? Charlie thought.

James agreed; she could feel it.

"And this task force will be well financed and given all opportunities to track down these people, yes? Including surveillance, access to whatever databases you have, intercepting communications..." Henry said.

The Home Secretary took off her glasses and placed them on the table in front of her.

"Subject to using the proper procedures. Nothing without a court order. I won't tolerate anyone cutting corners or trampling all over the rights and liberties of innocent people, just because someone has a hunch."

"I see." Henry's tone was guarded. Charlie couldn't make out if he was happy about the proposal or not.

An awkward silence filled the room.

"As a sign of good faith, I'm prepared to share something with you. But all this is off the record." The Home Secretary looked directly at Charlie now. "If this ends up in the papers tomorrow, the deal is off the table, you understand?"

Charlie put her pen down on the pad and held her hands up. "Off the record. No problem."

"The attacker that was taken in during the incident at Hyde Park. We offered him a deal, but only if he was willing to talk. It turns out he was able to track you down with the help of an old friend of yours."

Charlie frowned. Who could she be referring to?

"It turns out your former leader, Adrian Blacke, hates your movement so much he was willing to make a deal with the enemy. It seems he had an axe to grind with you personally, Mr. Finch," the Home Secretary's voice sounded almost triumphant. "We have him in custody. Considering what we found at his mansion in Stirling, it won't be difficult to keep him locked up for a long time."

"No way," Charlie whispered. She looked across at the others and saw they were equally shocked. The mention of Stirling, her home town, sparked her curiosity, though. Whatever they found there, she had to know. She would ask James about it later.

"This has been verified?" Henry asked.

"I'm afraid so." The Home Secretary cleared her throat. "I understand that we may find things there which will connect some of your people to what Blacke has been up to. Different times, shall we say. We're willing to overlook some of it, as long as everyone understands that those days are over."

Henry leaned back in his chair.

"This is a lot to take in, I understand. If you need time to think about it, that's fine," the woman said.

Charlie waited with bated breath. What would Henry say to all this? How would the New Alliance proceed?

"No need," Henry finally spoke up. "Your proposal for a joint task force is acceptable. My priorities lie with keeping my people safe. That's what our entire movement has been about from the beginning. We still have a long way to go before everyone accepts us for what we are."

Henry took a deep breath. "Now that Blacke is no longer a threat, we'll have to focus on Victor Domnall and his people. He will have gathered quite a bit of support, and although there may not be much activity right now, I've had the misfortune of dealing with his people for too long. As long as they're out there, they're planning something."

Charlie breathed a sigh of relief. This was the right way forward; she was certain of it.

"In that case, my people will be in touch when the groundwork has been laid. We'll arrange for an office and put forward a shortlist of human candidates. Please prepare a list of your own. They'll have to undergo some training to make sure they're aware of our laws and procedures."

"Of course," Henry said.

"Then we are all in agreement." The Home Secretary pushed her chair back, nodded at everyone present, and finally shook Henry's hand to symbolically seal the deal.

Charlie's head was spinning now. This was huge, though of course, she couldn't report on the entire last part of the conversation, but still.

She looked over at James, only to find his eyes already on her.

How about that, eh? Charlie thought.

He smiled. *We won. The New Alliance has won.*

She smiled back at him. It certainly did seem so.

Sure, they hadn't quite won everyone over yet. And the Sons of Domnall were still out there. But with shifter equality making its way into existing legislation, and this joint task force...

This was the way forward, and the future was bright.

– THE END –

ABOUT THE AUTHOR

Dear Reader,

Thanks for reading Scottish Werebear: A Second Chance, the 6th and final book in the Scottish Werebears Series. Fear not, though; if you're desperate for more werebear stories, you might want to check out my Alpha Squad series, a spin-off from the Scottish Werebears.

Although this was my first published paranormal romance series, I'm not new to writing in general. In fact, my mom still tells me to this day about how I would make up stories, and attempt to record them in my clumsy, shaky handwriting from the moment I learned to read and write. From there I went on to write fan fiction and other stuff meant for my own eyes only.

I've always enjoyed stories of the paranormal. Vampires, shape shifters, witches and magic, all featured in the books I loved the most, even when I was still growing up. But it wasn't until much later that I got into romance. One of the first writers (a self-published author just like me!) I came across was Tina Folsom, via her Scanguards Vampire series. I was hooked. From there I went on to read more paranormal romance until I found a new favorite kind of hero: bear shifters, like the kind written by Milly Taiden, Zoe Chant, and T.S. Joyce. What I love about bears is how they can be all strong and independent, a bit reclusive, and almost grumpy, but they always end up having a heart of gold (plus they tend to know their food, and we all know that a man who can cook is doubly sexy). All that (except for the shifting into a powerful bear) almost exactly describes the sort of man I ended up falling for and marrying in real life, so it's no surprise that this is what I started my publishing career with.

To find out more, check:
LoreleiMoone.com (And why not sign up for the newsletter to be the first to find out about new releases.)

You can also get in touch with me via Facebook (search for Lorelei Moone), or email at info@loreleimoone.com

I also write contemporary romance as L. Moone. If that's something you're interested in, you can take a look at LMoone.com.

x Lorelei